SECRET OF THE UNICORN

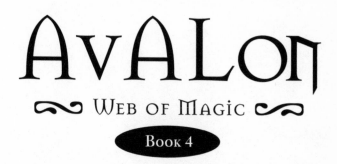

WEB OF MAGIC

BOOK 4

SECRET OF THE UNICORN

RACHEL ROBERTS

Seven Seas

SECRET OF THE UNICORN

Published by Seven Seas Entertainment.

ISBN: 978-1-933164-71-7

Cover and interior illustrations by Allison Strom

Interior book design by
Pauline Neuwirth, Neuwirth & Associates, Inc.

10 9 8 7 6 5 4 3 2

Printed in the USA

WOODS

WOODS

OWL CREEK
BIRD SANCTUARY

EAGLE RIDGE

OWL CREEK

DEER
MEADOW

BAMBOO
FOREST

PORTAL
FIELD

MIRROR
LAKE

MAGIC GLADE

HIDDEN FALLS TRAIL

SWAN LAKE
TRAIL

ROCKING
STONE

HEDGE
MAZE

SWAN LAKE

TURTLE
BOG

CHITAKAWAY RIVER

WOLF RUN
PASS

WATER
GARDEN

TOPIARY
GARDENS

ROSE
GARDENS

ADRIANE'S
HOUSE

SCULPTURE
GARDENS

RAVENSWOOD
MANOR

MIST TRAIL

MAIN GATE

STONE WALL

PLAYING
FIELDS

MAIN ROAD

1

*E*MILY FLETCHER DANCED.

Swirling, soft lights surrounded her as the melody carried her away. It was like no song she'd ever imagined—lyrical, dazzling, enchanting. Bathed in the sweet sounds, she longed for the song to go on forever. Snowflakes spun like crystalline notes, moving the music faster. The melody curved, arcing like a graceful bird, then fell like the sea, crashing to the shores in timeless rhythm. Arms outstretched, Emily twirled like a ballerina. Reaching for the dizzying notes, she felt the melody slipping away on snow-white silken wings. She ached for the music to find her again. Somehow she knew that she was the only one who had ever heard this song. It was part of her, something important that needed to be sung and she was the only one who could bring it to life.

THE DREAM WAS still as vivid as it had been when she'd awakened that morning. Summoning her memory of the song, Emily raised her flute and—

ScroooK!

That sure wasn't it. Furrowing her brow, Emily placed her fingers against the keys. Taking a deep breath, she lifted the mouthpiece to her lips and blew into the instrument again.

A series of lovely notes wafted into the air. Gaining confidence, she replayed the melody in her mind as her fingers flew faster toward the final phrase.

SKEoooW!

Emily wrinkled her nose. She turned the flute over in her hands. The cool metal felt smooth and sleek against her palms.

"That'll sure make an impression at the audition," she muttered, tossing a strand of loose, reddish-brown hair from her face. She glared at the flute, its clean lines and gleaming, polished surface catching sparkles of light from the large window in her bedroom. The beautiful instrument seemed to mock her weak, off-key attempts to play such an exquisite song. She glanced around her bedroom helplessly, wondering why she'd even bothered in the first place.

Don't drop the music because of me, her father had said over the phone the evening before. *That's really cool you're trying out for the jazz band.*

She hadn't bothered to explain that there was no jazz band at Stonehill Middle School, only a marching band—not that she'd thought one way or another about joining it. In fact, she hadn't even bothered to unpack her flute case until that very morning. Even though it had been almost a year since her parents had divorced and her whole world had broken apart, she still didn't feel much like making music. It was easier just to stick with every-day, necessary things—school, homework, helping her mother at the veterinary clinic—and now her involvement with the Ravenswood Wildlife Preserve and all the magical animals that lived there.

How could she explain that to her father, though? An enthusiastic amateur saxophonist, he had been thrilled when he'd realized that Emily had inherited his gift for music—right along with her mother's knack with animals. She remembered those lazy afternoons playing music together. Dad riffing on the sax, dancing around like a rock star, Emily tootling along on the flute. Mom always covered her ears, but Emily didn't care what they sounded like. The important thing had been sharing those moments—moments now faded like remnants of a tattered dream. Trying to reconnect with those feelings, she had taken out her once-prized possession. But now Emily couldn't seem to find the right notes. Her mind could no longer wrap around the music and flow with it. She felt the loss piling up inside, even as she tried so hard to keep it at bay. Maybe she once had musical talent, but that had changed.

That wasn't the only thing that had changed lately.

Emily held up her wrist and eyed the rainbow-colored stone on its beautiful silver bracelet. Nobody would have guessed that it was anything other than a pretty piece of jewelry. Only Emily and her friends, Kara Davies and Adriane Charday, knew the rainbow jewel had special powers. Together, the three of them had discovered magic—and the unique talents each of them had as mages—magic users.

Emily was a healer. She had helped dozens of injured magical animals who lived at Ravenswood by focusing her healing power with the rainbow jewel. Adriane was a warrior. The gem she had found looked like a tigereye, but ever since she bonded with the mistwolf called Stormbringer, she'd called it her wolf stone. She and Storm trained together tirelessly, learning to use their magic to enhance the warrior's speed, strength, and combat skills. Kara was a blazing star. Even though she didn't have a jewel, she could magnify the magic of others, attracting, strengthening, and sharpening it.

As if in response to her thoughts, the rainbow jewel caught a ray of light through the window and sparkled.

Too bad I can't magically remember how to play music, Emily thought, sighing.

She closed her eyes and let the warm sunlight dapple across her face as she thought about the dream. The notes of the song danced through her head again, haunting her like ghosts. Quickly, before they could slip away, she lifted the flute and played. The music poured easily out of the instrument, each note clear and shimmering. But as she neared the elusive end, the notes danced out of reach, and the melody faded. She paced her breathing, knowing what her father would say: *Follow the music, Em. Don't be afraid to really feel it.*

She couldn't let herself give up. She wasn't a quitter.

Closing her eyes tightly, she reached inside, trying to find the notes that would bring just the right ending. Her fingers moved to form a high C—no, not a C, it should be an *F sharp!* She hit the new note, blowing with all her might.

SooOOKKwHooONGGG!

A deafening cacophony of sound burst from the flute, like a dozen different chords being played at once on an enormous pipe organ.

Emily's eyes flew open. The notes hung in the air, vibrating and fighting one another, loud and jarring and clashing. Her flute was changing colors—gold, scarlet, amethyst, and emerald flashed across its polished surface, one after another, flowing like waves of color. The colors expanded and filled the room, glowing brighter and brighter with every passing second, until dark spots swam in front of Emily's eyes. She leaped to her feet, letting the flute fall to the thick beige carpet. Her jewel was flashing like a rainbow beacon.

And just like that, the colors blinked out and the sound stopped, as if someone had flipped a switch.

Emily blinked, trying to clear her vision.

A knock on the door broke through the sudden silence. "Emily?"

With a gasp, Emily jumped.

She hurried to the door and flung it open. Her mother stood in the narrow upstairs hallway, dressed in her veterinarian's lab coat, smiling wryly.

"Got the flute out, I hear." Carolyn Fletcher peered into the room curiously. "Sounded like a whole orchestra."

"Oh, uh, I was playing along with the radio," Emily lied breathlessly, sliding a long sleeve over her jeweled wrist. "Didn't realize it was so loud."

Carolyn nodded, handing Emily a sheet of paper. "My noon appointment's here, Doc," she said. "I need you to check this delivery. This order doesn't seem right."

Emily gawked at the shipping slip as if waiting for it to turn green.

"Now would be a good time," Carolyn added sternly.

With a flash of guilt, Emily looked over at the clock on her bedside table. "I guess I lost track of time."

"You've been doing that a lot lately." Carolyn raised an eyebrow. "I can't always be available to back you up when you get off schedule. Our guests in the Pet Palace can't feed themselves, you know."

"I know," Emily mumbled. "I'm sorry. I'm on it right now."

"And make sure those dogs get walked!" Carolyn called out.

"Okay!" Hurrying past her mother, Emily took the stairs two at a time and headed for the back door. The Pet Palace was located in an old barn behind the house. It had been Emily's idea, when they'd first moved to Stonehill that summer, to convert it into a kennel for boarding pets.

As Emily jogged across the short strip of lawn separating the house from the barn, she read over the delivery form. Two dozen bags of gourmet kibble, liver, beef, bacon, and mixed blend; eight boxes of special biscuits and treats; a box of jerky strips; two dozen snuggle toys; a pet bed heater; and a grooming kit?

That's a strange order, Emily thought. It looked like supplies for a pet *party*. She swung open the barn door, and her eyes widened in horror.

The kennel was a disaster. Large bags of pet food were flung everywhere. Near a row of open cages, Muffin, the Feltners' terrier, and Ranger, the Paulsons' shepherd mix were growling at each other as they played tug-of-war with a strip of beef jerky. The rear paws of a spotted beagle stuck out of a giant bag of gourmet kibble. A very contented Persian cat stared out from inside a box of treats.

"These liver snaps are delicious," a voice said around a mouth full of food.

Emily looked at the cat, eyes wide. "You can talk?"

"Of course I can talk! Pass some of that jerky."

Oh, no! She flashed back to the wild colors dancing across her flute, those bursts of weird sound in her room. Had she accidentally released some kind of crazy magic? She and her friends had learned a lot about how magic worked, but they still didn't know everything. Not even close.

"Easy, Maurice," she called softly, taking a step toward the cat. "How long have you been talking?"

Maurice blinked big green eyes. "Ever since I was a little elf."

A small, bright-eyed, furry face popped into view behind the cat. Two ferret eyes went wide in astonishment as they surveyed the barn. *"Gah!* I told you guys to put the stuff away! I didn't mean literally!"

So *that's* who'd been talking! "Ozzie." Emily crossed her arms and glared at the golden-brown ferret. "What's going on here?"

Ozzie shook his head. Then he hopped out of the kibble pile and, standing on his back paws, brushed crumbs off his belly. He had a small silver comb stuck in the fur behind his ears.

"What do you have to say for yourself?" Emily asked sternly.

"Uurrrp."

"Did you place this order?" She waved the shipping form in the ferret's face, forcing him to sit back.

Squeak!

"'Scuse me." Ozzie removed two snuggle toys from under his rump. "You said you needed help with the supplies, so I ordered some."

Emily put her hands on her hips and glared at him. She should have known. This wasn't a magical mishap at all. It was an Ozzie ferret fiasco.

Ozzie could pass as an ordinary ferret, as long as he didn't open his mouth to talk. He was really an elf from a magical world called Aldenmor. He had been sent to Earth by the Fairimentals, protectors of the good magic of Aldenmor, to search for three mages—a healer, a warrior, and a blazing star. They were destined to help find a mysterious place called Avalon, the legendary home of all magic. Ozzie had been upset to find that the Fairimentals had disguised him as a ferret to help him blend in on Earth. But he still managed to enjoy exploring everything this new world had to offer—especially the edible parts.

"I asked you to inventory supplies, not order the entire catalog!" Emily said, bending over to pull the jerky away from the struggling dogs.

Ozzie shrugged and kicked piles of loose kibble into a half-empty plastic package. "I inventoried. There was nothing left. Mmrrph, these liver snaps are especially tasty."

Emily watched him shove more food into his mouth. So much for having everything under control. As usual, control seemed to have slipped away from her when she was least expecting it.

"*Stoof!*" Ozzie spit out a piece of kibble. "Who ordered the rice and lamb flavor?"

"How am I going to explain this?" she grumbled, grabbing a broom. "Since you made this mess, the least you could do is help me clean up."

"Sure, no problem." He leaned hard against Scooter the beagle, trying to push the dog's nose away from the bag of kibble. "Ugh—move it!"

"We have to hurry." Emily started picking up boxes and bags. "I'm supposed to pick up Kara at the football game, then meet Adriane at Ravenswood."

Ozzie had resorted to jumping onto the dog's back. Scooter stood up, and Ozzie slid off with a "Whoa!" scattering more treats across the floor.

Scooter sat on Ozzie and licked the ferret's head.

"*Gak!*" Ozzie wriggled away.

Emily rolled her eyes. Obviously she was going to have to take care of things herself—and fast. If she didn't leave soon, she would be late meeting her friends.

Thinking about Kara and Adriane gave her an idea. She stared at her stone.

Could she do this? Moving objects around magically was Adriane's department, not hers. Still, what did she have to lose? "It's worth a shot, right?"

"Yes-*aahhk!*" The two other dogs were jumping excitedly up and down over Ozzie. "Hurry!" the ferret screamed.

Emily stared at the jewel on her wrist, focusing all her attention on it. Her breathing slowed. She lifted her eyes to a big bag of kibble and pictured it moving up into the air and over to one of the open food bins against the far wall. Her stone began to glow softly as she worked to visualize every detail—the bag lifting, swaying, and floating across the room.

At first she didn't think it was working. Taking a deep, cleansing breath, she willed herself to sink deeper into her own mind, concentrating totally on her goal. The room around her faded into a vague, misty background. Nothing existed except her and the bag.

The bag quivered, then slowly levitated a few inches into the air.

"I did it!" Emily cried. "It's moving!"

Psyched that her experiment was working so well, Emily refocused her energy. By using magic, she could have the whole place cleaned up in no time! The bag lifted higher . . . higher . . . Soon it was floating five feet above the floor.

"Okay," she murmured. "Now to move you over to the bins."

She traced an arc in the air with her gemstone, trying to steer the levitating bag toward the wall. The bag shuddered and bucked.

At the same time, her head was filled with a jangling,

discordant sound—awful, broken, painful notes just like her flute had made a few minutes earlier. These were stronger, though.

"Ruff!"

A chubby beagle floated by Emily's head.

"Uh-oh."

"Meow!"

There went Maurice!

Suddenly the barn was filled with flying animals, floating around the room in a whirl.

"Down!" Emily yelled out.

Kapow!

A bag of kibble under Ozzie exploded in a burst of rainbow light, so bright that Emily cried out and squeezed her eyes shut.

"Whubbaa!" Ozzie tumbled head over heels from the center of the explosion.

Emily felt tiny, hard objects pelt her head and shoulders like hail. Looking up and squinting cautiously through one eye, she saw sparkling pellets raining down all around her. As they hit the floor, they popped back into ordinary brown kibble.

As suddenly as it began, it all stopped. The animals were on the ground, no worse for the wear.

What had just happened? What was that awful noise?

Ozzie tottered over to Emily. "Are you okay?"

The healer shook her head, weird, jangling sounds echoing in her mind. "Something is very wrong."

2

"*H*EEL, SCOOTER!" EMILY cried.

The stout little beagle looked up at her uncomprehendingly, his pink tongue lolling happily out of his mouth. With a shrill *yip!* he bounced off in pursuit of a passing moth, tangling his leash around Ranger's legs. Muffin stopped suddenly, nose down, investigating a half-eaten hot dog.

"Aaaargh!" Emily tugged at the leashes, dragging the three dogs toward the playing fields behind the high school.

Just ahead, she could hear the cheers of a large crowd. Today was Stonehill Middle School's first big football game of the year, and it sounded as if half the town had turned out. It was just past noon. She hoped it was almost half-time. The sooner Kara's cheerleading was over, the sooner they could join Adriane at Ravenswood. Emily couldn't shake the feeling that something was wrong there and every minute she had to wait was a minute lost.

As Emily and her charges got closer, she heard the marching band start to play. They sound pretty good, she thought. Not like the lame band at my old school.

Hurrying forward and peering through a gap in the bleachers, she saw the band standing in formation on the sidelines on the far side of the field. As she turned away to check on the dogs, the band finished their song and started another. The last one had been a fight song, but this new one sounded—different. Emily listened in surprise, rooted to the spot. The instruments sounded muted and exotic, the complex and sinuous melody slithering its way into her mind like a snake. She blinked, and her eyelids felt strangely heavy and slow. Why did she suddenly feel so funny, like she was moving through water instead of air? The music crept into her mind, taking root—beautiful, haunting, incredible music. It sounded so familiar. Swinging her head around with effort, she stared at the marching band.

Wait . . . a . . . second, she thought, the words flowing through her mind like molasses. They're not even . . . playing their instruments . . . right now. Where . . . is that music . . . coming from?

"Rrrrrowrf!"

Emily snapped out of her daze as Scooter leaped forward, yanking the leash right out of her hand. "Hey!" she blurted as the little beagle raced toward a tall woman who was just turning away from the nearby hot-dog stand. "Oh no," she whispered as she recognized the woman.

Mrs. Beasley Windor let out a shriek as the beagle planted his muddy paws on her spotless beige slacks. "Off!" she yelled. "Get off of me, you mangy beast!"

"Oops!" Emily gasped, lunging forward and pulling the dog back by his collar. Scooter panted with excitement and struggled to escape again. "I'm so sorry, Mrs. Windor," she exclaimed.

"Well, little Miss Ravenswood Tour Guide." The woman glared at Emily over her beak of a nose. "I should have known."

Emily felt her cheeks burning. Of all the bad luck! Mrs. Windor was an influential member of the town council. She thought the Ravenswood Wildlife Preserve was a menace and wanted to develop the land into a county club. Emily and her friends had led the winning fight to save Ravenswood and had been appointed official tour guides for the wildlife sanctuary, much to Mrs. Windor's displeasure.

"I'm really sorry," Emily mumbled helplessly.

Mrs. Windor sniffed and said, "If this is how you watch those animals, it won't be long until someone gets hurt." She bent closer, her voice a cold hiss. "I know you and your friends were responsible for letting dangerous animals loose in the town. As soon as I can prove it, we'll just see how fast Mayor Davies changes his mind about your precious Ravenswood." She stood and scowled at Emily. "I'm keeping my eye on you."

With that, she stormed away toward the far end of the bleachers.

"Great. Just great," Emily muttered. The last thing she wanted to do was give Mrs. Windor any more ammunition in her campaign against Ravenswood. If the preserve was bulldozed, dozens of magical animals who secretly lived there—quiffles, pegasi, brimbees, and many others—would no longer have a safe haven. Not to mention the fact that Adriane's grandmother lived there as caretaker, and if Ravenswood was shut down, Adriane and Gran would lose their home.

Emily shuddered as she remembered the wrath in Mrs. Windor's beady little eyes when Scooter jumped up on her. Maybe bringing Pet Palace clients to the football game hadn't been such a hot idea after all.

Keeping a firm grip on the leashes, she headed into the gap between the two closest sets of bleachers. The marching band was playing again—a normal song, no weird snakelike melodies this time. She shifted her gaze to the faces of the spectators across the field. Where was Kara? A mass of golden hair fluttered. Was that her? Emily strained to look closer. The crowd seemed to fade away as one face crystallized and leaped out—and all the breath left her body in a *whoosh*.

Pale skin. Pale as death. Jagged, grotesque cheekbones. Skeletal shoulders draped in black. And the eyes—Emily

felt ice course through her veins as she caught a glimpse of two blazing pools of malice and evil. The ghoul suddenly looked straight at her and smiled with a wide, red-rimmed mouth full of crooked yellow teeth.

Emily squeezed her eyes shut. Her whole body had gone numb and cold. She felt a wave of dizzying nausea sweep over her. She wobbled forward, throwing her hands out just in time to stop herself from falling.

"Hey!" The teenage boy whose shoulder she'd grabbed was staring at her suspiciously as she opened her eyes. "What's the deal?"

"Um, sorry," Emily blurted, her gaze wandering back toward the ghastly specter.

But it was gone. She blinked, staring up at the bleachers. All sorts of people were sitting there, watching the game as if nothing out of the ordinary had happened. The horrid skeletal face was nowhere to be seen.

Emily shot another cautious glance across the field. Had she really seen that thing, or was her imagination playing tricks on her?

This was getting really weird. The rainbow jewel on her silver bracelet pulsed a steady warm glow as feelings of dread tickled up and down her back. She had to find Kara and get to Ravenswood fast. She took a step forward when Muffin and Ranger leaped out in front of her, nearly sending her head over heels again.

"Look who's here," a familiar voice said. "It's Ms. Dolittle, the animal girl."

Glancing up, Emily found herself looking straight into the grinning face of Kara's fourteen-year-old brother, Kyle. Kara's friends Molly, Heather, Tiffany, Joey, and Marcus were sitting with him.

"Oh." Emily gulped, disentangling herself from the dogs' leashes. She was suddenly way too aware of her flushed, sweaty face, her messy hair, and the dogs drooling on her shoes. Stay calm, she told herself. "Um, hi, guys."

"More comfortable to *sit* and watch the game," Marcus commented, sliding over to create a space next to him and Joey.

"Thanks." Emily felt herself blush as she sat down on the bench. "Are you okay?" she asked, pointing to the splint on Marcus's right wrist.

"Sure. Just a sprain, but enough for Coach Berman to keep me out of play for a week," Marcus grimaced.

"Just when Stonehill needs 'Marcus the Sharkus!'" Kyle slapped his friend on the shoulder. "Emily's the doc, maybe she can do her magic on you. Whatdaya say, Em?"

"I'm only good with animals," she responded, hardly paying attention. She anxiously scanned the field for Kara.

Joey broke out in a laugh, punching Marcus in the arm. "Exactly."

Emily smiled in spite of her worry. They weren't bad kids, just silly. She leaned forward to pat the shepherd as it sat down by her feet. The other two dogs sprawled on the grass in front of Marcus.

"Hey, Ranger," Marcus said, kneeling forward to tickle the shepherd behind the ears. Ranger gave the boy a big, slobbering lick. Kyle and Joey jumped down to play with the other dogs. The dogs barked in pleasure, crowding in for some petting time.

Marcus was sprawled on the grass with Ranger. "You do a great job at that pet hotel."

"Thanks." Emily smiled, trying to hide the fear building inside.

"Who brings all their *pets* to a football game anyway?" Heather asked snidely.

Emily bit her lip.

"Where's Adriane? Is she coming to the game?" Joey asked.

"She's over at Ravenswood," Emily answered.

Marcus snickered. "Dude, you are way too obvious." He winked at Emily.

As the others turned their attention to the game, Emily gazed across the field to where she'd seen that ghastly face. Or had she? After the way she'd spaced out just before Scooter started jumping all over Mrs. Windor, she wasn't too sure. She snuck a peek at her jewel. The stone now lay quietly on her bracelet. She frowned, remembering the flute and the flying dogs. Had she imagined all that, too? No way.

"Yeah, but Emily here could save the day." Molly's voice broke into Emily's thoughts. "She's got enough animals for five schools."

"She's like a walking zoo," Heather sniffed.

"Yeah, smells like one, too," Tiffany muttered just loud enough for Emily to hear.

"Huh?" Emily belatedly realized that she had become the topic of conversation again. "Um, what did you say?"

Tiffany shrugged and examined her perfectly manicured nails. "Keep up, animal girl. We were just saying how lame it is that we don't have a team mascot," she explained lazily. "That's totally got to be why we're losing this game."

A glance at the scoreboard confirmed it. The home team was down by six points, with less than two minutes left on the clock before half-time. She looked at the person in a tiger costume dancing around on the sidelines near the end zone.

"Wait," she said. "If Stonehill doesn't have a mascot, what's with the guy in the stripes down there?"

Heather snorted. "That's the *other* team's mascot," she exclaimed. "They're the Thornbury Tigers. We're the Stonehill Sparks. Duh."

"Whatever," Emily muttered, sorry she'd said anything. Still, she could look on the bright side—a couple of weeks earlier, Heather and Tiffany wouldn't have bothered to speak to her at all. They had been best friends with Kara for years. And now Kara was spending so much of her time hanging out with relatively uncool Emily and Adriane. How would Kara explain it? *You see, the three of us are mages destined to save the universe and find the source of all magic.* Right. That would go over *really* well.

Still, Kara had done an amazing job getting her old friends involved in helping out with the tours. Ravenswood needed all the friends it could get. Emily hid a smile as she glanced out onto the field, where both teams were huddling.

"How about the Sparky the Stonehill Beagle?" Kyle spoke up. "Go Beagles!" He stood up and howled.

"Sit down, you goof," Molly commanded, yanking at the hem of his rugby shirt.

"His name is Scooter—" Emily's words were cut off as the marching band launched into a loud, rousing fight song. Kara and the other cheerleaders raced onto the field, dancing along with the music, their blue-and-gold pompoms tracing out patterns in the air.

Emily winced. Was it just her or was the band's music painfully loud? A hard, sharp high note blared at her, seeming to travel directly from the trombone section to her eardrums. She shook her head as the flutes broke in shrilly, their unrelenting tones piercing through her consciousness until she couldn't think straight.

Glancing at the others, Emily saw that they seemed totally unaware of what was happening. Why couldn't they hear it? She cringed as a cymbal crash reverberated through her bones and made her teeth chatter. Only the dogs seemed to notice that anything was wrong. All three of them were sitting up and whining nervously.

Emily was vaguely aware of a creeping feeling, pulling at the edges of her mind. Suddenly a saxophone punched out a series of harsh, off-key notes, sounding as if it was wailing directly in her ear, and she gasped.

"Em? Hey, you okay? You look kind of weird." Marcus stared at her.

Emily squeezed her eyes shut. The sounds were too painful for her to answer.

Everyone except Emily suddenly leaped to their feet. The kids were yelling as the Stonehill team pushed forward to the twenty-yard line.

The cheers echoed as if in a huge cavern. Emily shook her head again, trying to clear it. "I—I'm okay." But she knew she wasn't. Fear trickled up and down her back.

The others weren't even listening to her anymore. There was a sudden flurry of movement on the field, and another roar went up from the crowd.

A wave of pain lanced through her, but her scream was covered in the raucous cheers around her.

"Score!" Joey crowed, pumping his fist in the air. "Now all we need is a field goal, and we could actually win this thing!"

"Check it out!" Heather's voice was shrill with excitement. "Someone's starting the wave over there."

Emily gasped for breath. The band had reached a fever pitch, and the cheerleaders were going crazy with excitement. As if in a dream, she saw Kara bounce into a high kick as some of the other girls started to form a pyramid on the sidelines.

"Kara," Emily whispered, doubling forward as sharp cramps wracked her body.

Kara jumped to a stop, startled. She looked around the stands, her long blond hair flying in the wind.

"Kara . . ." It was all Emily could do to keep from screaming out. "Help me."

Across the way, the crowd was cheering and hollering as it performed the wave, the people in each section of the bleachers standing and waving their arms in turn. The human wave traveled swiftly from the left end of the bleachers to the right, then jumped across the field to the far end of Emily's side. She could see it coming . . . closer . . . closer.

The band was playing faster and louder than ever. Emily clenched her hands into fists, her face wet from sweat and tears. Her heart beat faster and faster as her wrist burned fire. Her jewel was blazing in warning.

Marcus, Joey, and the others jumped up, shouting and throwing their hands into the air. But Emily couldn't move, bound by the oppressive weight of overwhelming pain. She swallowed hard, closed her eyes tight, and braced for the impact as the enormous tidal wave of magic energy smashed into her. The rainbow jewel exploded with color, and everything went black.

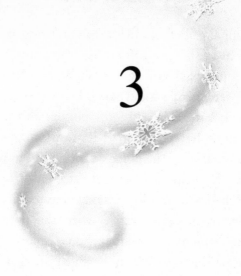

3

*T*HE SOUND RUMBLED across the field like an incoming train. Lightning sparked, even though the day was clear. Three electrical bolts slammed together in an explosion of light and sound. An immense dark cloud swirled out of nothingness as the air split open.

The portal hovered in the air just above the field at Ravenswood.

Animals and creatures came tumbling out, falling over one another in a rush as they hit the ground.

"Warrior, come quickly!" Storm called to Adriane. The mistwolf was already bounding across the field to help the new arrivals move away from the portal before it could close and vanish.

Wails of pain filled the field. Adriane's breath caught in her throat as she ran in from the surrounding woods to witness the chaos and confusion. Bodies, furred and feathered, were scorched and covered with a sickly green glow—Black Fire. The dreadful poison of the Dark Sorceress must be spreading. If it wasn't stopped, the magical world called Aldenmor would be laid to waste.

Lyra, the large spotted, winged cat bonded to Kara, and Ariel, the snow owl, had been among the first wave of wounded creatures to arrive when the portal first appeared that summer. Since then, no new refugees from Aldenmor had arrived. Today changed all that. Now, dozens of hurt and dying creatures were struggling to reach the safety of Ravenswood.

Just as the last arrivals were herded off to the side, the portal began to close. Suddenly, another creature appeared in the shrinking, swirling hole. It screeched in fear, a wild, jumbled sound. Bright colors shimmered across its body as it darted from the closing portal, bolted into the woods, and vanished.

"EMILY, ARE YOU all right?"

"Is she dead?"

"You doofus. She fainted!"

Voices reached her from down a long hallway. Emily felt rough dirt and grass against her cheeks. Then she felt hands lifting her up as she opened groggy eyelids. She looked into the concerned faces of Marcus, Joey, and Molly. Kyle, Heather, and Tiffany sat behind them, watching.

"Are you all right, Emily?" Marcus asked.

She could see why Kara liked this boy; he had such deep blue eyes, full of compassion.

"I—uh—fine." She tried to push away, but her hands didn't seem to understand her brain's command. Instead she clung tightly to Marcus's arm.

"Move it. Move it. I said out of the way!"

The sound of Kara's voice sent Emily's strange sense of serenity skittering away. The golden-haired girl pushed her way to Emily's side, taking half her weight from Marcus.

Emily shook her head, trying to gather her thoughts. That weird, snaky music was still dancing around somewhere in the far corners of her brain, distracting her and making her thoughts difficult to gather. She noticed other kids gawking with curiosity. The noise of the crowd suddenly flooded around her like a dam bursting.

"Man, you see that?"

"A girl passed out!"

"Give her some air."

"Is she all right?"

"Fine, fine," Kara replied to the gathered throng. "Bad hot dog."

Kara and Marcus gently settled Emily back on the bleacher seat. Joey handed her a bottle of water.

"Thank you," Emily said, taking a sip.

"What happened?" Kara asked.

"She just fainted," Marcus told her.

Emily winced. A rush of immense suffering washed over her. She recognized the feeling. Her mind raced back to one fateful August afternoon, only a few months ago. Lyra had been so badly burned that Carolyn had thought she would not survive. But Emily had helped Lyra heal, even before she had her rainbow jewel.

Suddenly everything became clear, the one possible explanation for what was happening: More injured creatures were coming through from Aldenmor. Their terror and distress pulsed at her like a beacon—a cry for help, for a healer.

"We have to get to Ravenswood right now," Emily told Kara, trying to stay calm in front of the other kids. "Animals are hurt."

"Lyra?" Kara asked worriedly.

"No. New ones."

"Healing animals is your thing, I have a game to win."

"We need you, too, Kara."

Kara looked back and forth between the cheerleaders and Emily's concerned face.

Ring, ring!

Kara whipped out a small pink cell phone from her waist cinch. "Hello?"

She listened for a few seconds, her sparkling blue eyes widening in shock. Then she snapped the phone shut. "Adriane," she said to Emily. "You're right."

She turned to her friends. "Listen up, you guys. We have a Ravenswood crisis. I have to go."

"Is there anything we can do to help?" Molly asked.

"Tell the others I had to leave."

"We'll take the dogs back to the Pet Palace for you," Marcus offered Emily.

"Thanks," Emily said, handing him the leashes. She gave him a grateful look.

Marcus smiled at her.

Emily felt herself pulled away as Kara grabbed her arm. "Let's go."

The two girls raced down the sidelines heading toward the exit.

4

STORMBRINGER'S KEEN EYES spotted Emily and Kara as they pushed through a patch of woods toward the huge, grassy expanse where the portal had appeared at the Ravenswood Preserve. As they emerged into the meadow, the giant silver mistwolf raced up to them, skidding to a stop in front of Emily. *"Healer, come quickly."* Emily heard Storm's voice clearly in her mind.

Behind Storm, Lyra padded over to Kara. *"A new group of animals came through. They're in bad shape."*

Although Lyra was thinking her words at Kara, Emily could hear them, too. Fear gripped her heart. It was always this way when she got close to a creature that needed her. Its pain, fear, and confusion became her own, taking hold inside her and connecting her to the injured one. It was the hardest part of being a healer—having to share all those terrible feelings. Now she stared out over the meadow, her feet rooted to the ground in shock and horror.

It was worse than she had feared. Creatures of various sizes and shapes lay sprawled in the tall grass, crying and shaking. A pegasus stood forlornly, his hide covered with burns, one of his gauzy, butterflylike wings hanging at an unnatural angle, limp and torn. Two or three long-eared, deerlike jeeran staggered, their soft, green-striped fur charred and their skin oozing blood. There were many species Emily couldn't even identify—small red bearlike creatures, jet-black possum creatures—but their feelings of pain were all too familiar.

They were covered with patches of a sickly greenish glow, the unmistakable sign of the Dark Sorceress's hideous Black Fire. Its dark energy seeped into Emily's mind, making her feel light-headed.

A winged shape momentarily blocked the early afternoon sun as Ariel swooped from the sky and fluttered onto Emily's arm, wings sparkling with magical highlights of turquoise and jade. "Ooooh," the owl sighed sadly as she surveyed the scene.

Ariel had been the first creature Emily had ever healed by herself, and seeing the healthy shine of the snow owl's feathers bolstered Emily's courage. "I'm glad you're here," she said, hugging the owl close.

"Emily!" Adriane ran into the field, followed by Ozzie,

Balthazar the pegasus, and Ronif and Rasha, silver-billed ducklike creatures called quiffles. These magical animals had proved valuable advisors to the girls over the past few months.

Baby quiffles poked their heads out of pockets in Adriane's down vest. "Tell us what to do," the dark-haired girl asked Emily.

Emily snapped out of her daze. She looked at the ring of friends waiting for her. She wasn't doing anyone any good standing there staring. It was time to help.

Her first instinct was to run to the nearest injured creature and just dive right in. But a voice in her head—her mother's calm, cool, unhurried voice—warned otherwise. *Take the time to get organized. Don't move faster than you can think, or you'll end up working twice as hard and helping half as well.*

"Start figuring out who is worst off," she instructed her friends, working to keep her voice calm and assured. "Bring me those first. But keep the others near so I can get to them as fast as possible. Move the healed ones out of the way as soon as I'm done with them."

The entire group whirled into action. Within seconds Kara was hustling back over to Emily, ushering forward a badly burned red koala-sized bear. "Start with him." She patted the small, furry bear before hurrying away.

"Easy, there," Emily said, calming the scared creature. "Any idea what it is, Ozzie?"

"A wommel. They live in the trees of the Moorgroves."

Emily stared at the creature. It was keening softly, its big, wide eyes glazed over with pain. Out of the corner of her eye, she spotted Adriane herding a small group of limping, burned jeeran toward her. Did she have the strength to do this?

"It's going to be okay, little one," she murmured, placing a gentle hand on its soft, furry chest. Her rainbow jewel flashed erratically, cycling through colors.

She took a deep breath and forced herself to be still, to allow the wommel's pain to flow into her. Her stone pulsed in time with her heartbeat, and after a moment she became aware of the creature's heartbeat, fast and panicky beneath her hand. She breathed deeply and steadily, and gradually its heartbeat slowed, locking onto hers. Emily focused on the wommel's injuries and concentrated on sending out healing magic. The rainbow jewel blazed with light, and soon she could feel the Black Fire's poison weakening, breaking up—and leaving the creature's body. The sickly green glow faded, dissolving into rainbow sparkles that floated away on the breeze.

Emily barely had time to point the healed wommel toward Ozzie before the next victim arrived—and the next, and the next. For a while she could hardly even think, which was just as well. She had never seen so much horror and heartbreak all in one place. It seemed that the parade of injured creatures would never end.

Finally, Emily found herself healing the last of the

injured. Her knees wobbling, she sank to the ground, the dry seed heads of the autumn grass tickling her hands as she leaned back and felt the slight breeze cooling the sweat from her brow. Still, she couldn't quite seem to relax. A tiny nagging hint of something—a sound?— tickled the edges of her mind, like a teasing memory. But what was it? She wrinkled her nose and shook her head, but the vague sense of uneasiness remained.

Ozzie scampered up to Emily. "You did an amazing job. Who would have thought when I first met you that you would be the perfect healer mage I was looking for!" The ferret beamed with pride.

"Thanks, Ozzie," she said distractedly. Something was buzzing in her ear. Climbing to her stiff, tired legs with a groan, Emily glanced around the meadow once more, trying to pinpoint where the sound was coming from. But nothing she saw gave her an answer, so she just shrugged and followed Ozzie over to where her friends were standing among a kaleidoscope of creatures.

"Does anyone hear that?" she asked.

"Hear what?" Kara panted as she jogged over with Lyra.

Another wave of frenzied, broken, tuneless noise swept through Emily, like needles of sound piercing her all over. "That!" she gasped. "Those sounds. Can't you hear it?"

Adriane shot her a concerned glance. "What does it sound like?"

"Like—like an instrument badly out of tune."

"You're probably just exhausted." Kara smiled briefly at Emily, then turned and clapped her hands for attention. "Is that everyone?" she called. "Does anyone else need help? Speak up, guys."

"We're all better," the red wommel spoke. "Thank you, healer!"

"Yes, thank you, healer!" More creatures echoed the wommel's gratitude as a cheer rose up over the meadow.

"You were incredible," Adriane said to Emily.

"Yeah, really," Kara agreed.

Emily gave them a tired smile. A few worried mumbles from a handful of quiffles caught her attention. They were gathered around Ronif.

"You heard it, too?" one quiffle asked another.

"Where did it go . . . must be hurt really bad . . . too dangerous . . ."

Emily stepped toward the quiffles. "What are they saying, Ronif?"

"There might be another wounded creature, healer," the quiffle answered.

"Where?"

Ronif edged a little quiffle forward. "Tell them what you know, Waldo."

The quiffle called Waldo shrugged. "I think there was another, healer," he said, flapping his rubbery silver beak. "It was making horrible sounds."

"Sounds?" Emily echoed. She felt a chill trickle down her spine. "Ariel, did you see anyone else?"

"Something runs, hidden."

"What kind of creature?" Emily asked Waldo as Adriane, Kara, Stormbringer and Lyra walked over to join her.

Before the quiffle could say anything more, a newly arrived pooxim—a sleek little creature that looked like a cross between a songbird and a rabbit—spoke up in a singsong voice. "I *see*-saw it," the pooxim announced. "A *glim*-gleaming blue thing with *flish*-flashing angry eyes full of magic."

"Did anyone else see this magic creature?" Adriane asked.

"There was something behind us, following us!" another wommel cried excitedly. "We barely got away from it. It tried to run us over."

"But it wasn't blue," Waldo said. "It was green. It nearly kicked my head off."

"You're both wrong," a pegasus piped up. "It was a big purple beastie."

"No, it was red," a quiffle disagreed. "And it was howling so horribly I almost lost my mind—and my eardrums."

"Wait a second." Emily held up a hand. "Waldo said the creature was green, and the pooxim said blue. But the one you saw was red? Are you sure?"

The pegasus shrugged his sleek, spotted shoulders. "It

was so hectic when we came through the portal. Maybe I can't be sure of the color, but the sounds it made were unforgettable."

"Maybe it was something evil," a wommel suggested nervously.

At that moment, the noise came again, filling Emily's head. She clenched her fists hard, her fingernails digging into her palms. Glancing down at her stone, she saw that it was glowing with soft, multicolored light. She chewed on her lower lip. Her uneasiness was growing. She didn't think it was evil she was sensing—just uncertainty and suffering.

"There's another creature out there," she murmured aloud.

Ozzie looked at her. "Sounds like a lot of creatures."

"And it—they—also sound wild," Adriane added.

"It's hurt bad and needs help." Emily took a step toward the forest. "I'm going to check the woods."

Adriane grabbed her arm. "You are not going out there by yourself."

"What am I, chopped rugamug?" Ozzie straightened up to his full sixteen-inch height.

"No offense, Ozzie."

"It could be dangerous," he said.

"Right," Emily agreed quickly. "That's why you're coming with me. It's okay, Adriane," she continued. "You stay and get things organized here."

"Take Storm with you," Adriane ordered.

The great silver wolf rubbed against Emily's side, her ears pricked alertly.

"Thanks, Storm." Emily cast a glance at the forest surrounding the meadow. Even in broad daylight, the thick, tangled trees looked gloomy and forbidding. Whatever was out there needed help—needed her. With a deep breath, Emily headed into the woods.

5

"*F*OUR, FIVE . . ." KARA was counting off a group of jeeran, making notes on a pad so the creatures could be logged into the Ravenswood journals. She looked up as Adriane approached.

"How's it going?" the dark-haired girl asked.

"Eight, nine . . ." Or was that the same one she'd already counted? "Aargh!" Kara cried as she completely lost track of where she was.

"Everyone is settling in," Adriane announced. "Thank goodness Emily got here in time."

"One, two, three . . . Hey, you! Stand still!"

Adriane was glaring at her.

"Six, seven . . . what?" Kara demanded.

"I think we should contact Zach."

Kara smirked. A few weeks ago, Adriane had followed Stormbringer through the portal to Aldenmor. She'd had an amazing adventure there. But since her return, she refused to talk about the time she had spent with the adorable sandy-haired guy she'd met there. Emily and Kara were dying for details.

"Need a last-minute date to the harvest dance?" Kara asked innocently.

Adriane rolled her eyes. "Get real, Princess Pea Brain," she snapped. "I just think we should try to find out what's going on over there. Something caused the portal to open again, and these injuries were really awful."

Kara had to admit she had a point. "Okay. I can do that." She grinned. "What would you do without me?"

"Just call them." Adriane frowned. "Though why they listen to *you* is anyone's guess."

"It's all in the training." Kara took a deep breath, picturing the tiny, brightly colored dragonflies in her mind.

"Yoo-hoo!" she sang out. "Goldie, Barney, Fiona, Fred, Blaze! Come out, come out, wherever you are!"

A cloud of multicolored bubbles danced into sight. The bubbles burst in a sudden blizzard of flashing rainbow sparkles, turning into chirping, brightly colored flying mini-dragons.

"Kaa-raaa!" a golden one sang. It fluttered up and down happily before coming to rest on Kara's shoulder.

"Goldie!" As Kara scratched the little dragon's head, Goldie's golden, jeweled eyes glowed with pleasure.

Red Fiona, orange Blaze, and purple Barney vied for her other shoulder. "Kee Keee!"

"Dee-deee!" Blue Fred hooted gleefully, zipping around Adriane's head, leaving little trails of colored sparkles behind.

"Listen up, crew," Kara commanded sternly. "We have work to do."

The dragonflies perked up and sprang to attention.

"We need a little portal," Adriane said. "Like the one you made for me on Aldenmor."

"So start spinning," Kara ordered.

Moments later, the dragonflies had joined wingtips and were spinning in a perfect little circle.

"Good dragonflies," Kara said.

"Ooooo," Barney cooed.

"Show us where Zach is," Adriane said, picturing the boy's handsome face and warm smile, the way his eyes danced. "He has that dragon stone I gave him. Hone in on its magic."

"Ooookayy."

A swirling, wavering mist appeared inside the circle of spinning dragonettes. Adriane clutched her wolf stone with a look of intense concentration.

"Are you getting anything?" Kara peered into the small window anxiously. The dragonflies could be restless and unpredictable, and they were being asked to make strong magic. She knew they only had a few minutes to make contact.

Adriane shook her head in frustration. "Lyra, we need your help!"

The cat loped toward them. *"Rasha, Ronif, Balthazar, bring the others, too."*

The pegasus and two quiffles came, as did a dozen other animals drawn by the urgency in Lyra's voice.

Kara gestured for them to come closer. With all of their friendly magical energy joining in, Adriane's stone glowed brighter. She looked at Kara and held out her wrist. Kara reached out and touched her fist to Adriane's, making the wolf stone flare with amber light.

The mist within the portal swept away, replaced by a new, slightly hazy scene. The background details were blurry, like faded watercolors, but Zach's sharp-featured face stood out clear and unmistakable in the foreground.

"Adriane?" he asked uncertainly, blinking toward them. "Is that you?"

"It's me!" Adriane called. "How are you?"

"Fine. My dragon stone just went crazy," Zach said, holding up the bright red jewel on his wrist. Crimson facets sparkled like tiny flames. "I knew it was you."

"Hi." Kara's head pressed close to Adriane's.

"Hello."

Adriane glowered. "You remember Kara."

"Yes." But his eyes were on Adriane.

"How's Drake?" she asked, referring to the baby dragon Zach was raising on Aldenmor.

There was a sudden thunderous, roaring sound in the background. "What's that noise? Are you in trouble?"

"No, no, it's okay," Zach assured her quickly. "Drake is fine. He's really getting big and he misses you. Did all those animals make it to you safely?"

"Totally!" Kara called back. "It was a regular Noah's ark."

Zach and Adriane looked at Kara.

"Oops, sorry," Kara whispered. "You two kids go right ahead. This is a long-distance call. Pretend I'm not even here."

"Just tell us what happened," Adriane said.

As Zach opened his mouth to speak, his face swam woozily and his voice suddenly faded, as if the volume on a radio had just been turned way down.

"Hey!" Kara said sharply to the dragonflies. "Keep spinning!"

"KOookoo!" the dragonflies sang excitedly, spinning faster and faster. "Soo-reeeeeee!"

Zach's face swam back into clear view. " . . . another explosion near the Dark Sorceress's lair, " he was saying. "The biggest one yet."

"Is that how all the animals got burned?" Adriane asked.

Zach nodded. "Black Fire came down all over the place," he reported grimly. "But that's not all—whatever the Sorceress did made the portals here go wild. The one leading to Earth opened, and a bunch of others just suddenly disappeared—including all of the ones to the Fairy Glen."

"Oh, no!" Adriane gasped. This was seriously bad news. The Fairy Glen was the home of the Fairimentals and the magical heart of Aldenmor. "Have you tried to contact the Fairimentals?"

"Of course. But we haven't been able to find—"

His face wavered again. The dragonflies' bright wings were flickering wildly as they spun, letting out tiny popping noises and rainbow colored sparks.

"Wrap it up," Kara muttered to Adriane.

Adriane bit her lip.

" . . . you have to be careful," Zach was saying. "One of the mistwolves said he saw a suspicious creature go through the portal. He said it reeked of evil."

"Evil," Adriane breathed, tensing. "Did he say what *kind* of creature?"

Zach shook his head. "It went through too fast. Just be on the lookout."

"Okay, thanks." Adriane said.

"Adriane, I'm real glad to see you," Zach said.

"Me, too."

"I—"

"Me, too," Adriane smiled and blushed.

Zach grinned back

"How cute is this?" Kara said with a sugary smile. "Just make sure she's home by ten!"

At that moment, the dragonflies flew apart in a flurry

of squawks and chitters. The portal blinked out of existence.

"You ditz!" Adriane yelled. "Didn't you hear what he said?"

"Dragon stone, huh! How come *he* has a magic jewel?"

"Forget the stone! Something evil might have snuck in when the portal opened!" Adriane exclaimed.

"Oh, that."

"And it's loose out there," Adriane finished.

Together the girls turned their gaze to the edge of the glade. Beyond the tall firs that encircled the glade, an ocean of trees stretched into the blackness of deep forest.

A monster. And Emily was out in the woods tracking it down right now!

6

"I'VE FOUND ANOTHER *print, Healer.*"

Emily hurried to peer over Stormbringer's shoulder. A patch of sunlight illuminated a hoofprint pressed into the moist dirt near the edge of the path. The mist-wolf had already discovered half a dozen similar prints, beginning at the edge of the woods back in the meadow.

"Same size and shape as the others," Emily mused, studying the print. "Could be jeeran." She leaned closer as the faintest hint of sound flashed through her. Music? No, more like those off-kilter chords she'd heard earlier. She listened closely, but the sound was gone, leaving behind a lingering sense of anguish and defeat.

Ozzie stepped forward and peered at the print. "Jerran are stupid herd beasts with little magic. I still say pegasus," he guessed. "Or maybe something like a centaur or even a large kelpie. What do you think, Storm?"

Instead of answering, Storm stood stock-still, her limbs rigid and her eyes half closed. The tip of her bushy tail twitched slightly.

"What is it?" Emily asked anxiously.

Storm remained silent for several more seconds. Finally, she blinked her golden eyes and gazed at Emily somberly. *"The warrior just sent me a message,"* she said.

Adriane and the mistwolf shared such a strong bond that they could communicate mind to mind across almost any distance. "What did she say?"

"She has contacted Aldenmor," Storm told her. *"Something evil may have crossed over with the others."*

Emily felt a chill pass through her as she glanced down at the print again. One thing they had learned since discovering magic was that evil could take many forms. Something horrible could be out here with them right now. Behind a tree, listening to them, waiting . . . She took a step closer to Storm, drawing comfort from the mistwolf's powerful presence.

Ozzie looked worried. "What if we're following a satyr?"

"A what?" Emily asked.

Storm snuffled derisively. *"A satyr hardly warrants dangerous,'"* she said. *"They are mischievous troublemakers, healer, half goat and half goblin. More of a nuisance than anything."*

"How about a nightmare then?" Ozzie declared excitedly. "Big steeds black as night, snorting fire. One can take out a dozen trolls all by itself and—"

"The tracks head this way," Emily broke in. "Let's keep going. Whatever it is, we need to find it."

"Right," Ozzie muttered, breaking into a jog to keep up with the much longer legs of the others. "Unless, of course, it's a basilisk, in which case our best plan of attack might be to run very, very fast in the opposite direction."

Storm shot the ferret a glance. *"Mistwolves fear nothing,"* she reminded him. *"Not even basilisks."*

"Oh, yeah?" Ozzie retorted. "Well, ferrets—er, I mean, elves—fear nothing, either. Cousin Brommy took on a golem all by himself—tricked it into falling down a ravine. And golems are much tougher than your average evil creature."

"Golems are strong, ugly, and brutal, but not very intelligent," Storm agreed. *"Werebeasts, on the other hand . . ."*

"Werebeasts! Now *those* are monsters!" Ozzie agreed "And you don't die if one rips you to pieces—you just turn onto a creeping, howling, bloodthirsty, were—"

"Do we really have to talk about this right now?" Emily interrupted. Their conversation was starting to spook her. She was seriously hoping to avoid running into anything that fit into the evil, creepy, and larger than Storm category.

"It is best to know the enemy one is facing, healer," Storm said, sniffing the air near a thick stand of trees.

Emily flashed on the image of the ghastly face she'd seen at the football game but shook it off quickly. "I just think we—*ahh!*" She almost doubled over as a sudden burst of magic energy barreled into her like a punch in the gut. Colored lights ignited in her brain like flash-bulbs; blue, red, gold streaked across her vision like shooting stars.

Storm was at her side in an instant.

"Emily, what's wrong?" Ozzie's worried face looked up at her.

Wheezing, she glanced around. "Look!" she gasped.

She pointed to a break in the trees just ahead.

Flash! A streak of bright blue flickered behind a cluster of evergreens.

"Over there!" Ozzie yelled, pointing in a different direction.

Flash!

Emily whirled around. A short distance away, between two tree trunks, a burst of vivid red appeared.

Flash! This time, clear yellow.

Suddenly a screeching sound echoed off the rocks and leaves. It was all around them, coming from everywhere and nowhere. Emily slapped her hands over her ears. "That noise!"

Storm was tense, ears alert, tail straight out behind her, hackles rising.

The sounds built to a crescendo, piercing the woods like a hurricane, and then vanished, eerily echoing away into silence. Emily straightened up and took a deep breath.

"Which way did they go?" Ozzie cried, spinning around wildly. "Where are they?"

Emily spun around, too, trying to find the colors.

Flash! A hint of emerald green disappeared over a hillock farther down the trail.

"That way." Storm set off down the path at a brisk trot. Ozzie scampered after her, chattering about a color-changing enchanted gnome he'd once known.

Emily lagged behind, still breathing hard. The burst of magic she'd felt had been so sudden, so powerful. And that sound . . .

What *was* that sound?

Her steps slowed. Wrinkling her brow, she gazed around and strained to hear. Gradually she became aware of sweet tones singing in her ears, beautiful, exotic music that floated into her head as easily as if it had always been there, always belonged there. Where . . . is . . . that . . . coming . . . from? Emily wondered, stopping in her tracks. She hardly noticed that Storm and Ozzie were almost out of sight ahead of her. She had to hear more.

She started to turn, swaying as the music wrapped around her. Arms outstretched, she weaved from side to side. Streams of sunlight fell in patterns of shifting light and shadows as the sweet sound snuck into her head. That melody, so enchanting, teasing, reaching out to her.

Leaves tumbled around her as she danced through sunbeams.

Something was moving with her. It was between two large trees. She couldn't put her finger on exactly what it might be—its face and body were vague. All she could focus on was its eyes. Deep, dark pools of bliss, watching her. They seemed to hold all the love, wisdom, and certainty of the world. Within those eyes, nothing changed—ever. All was still, calm, perfect . . .

"Come clossserrr . . ."

The words were barely a whisper in her mind, a graceful counterpoint to the haunting melody that surrounded her. Feeling as if she existed in some wonderful, never-ending dream, Emily danced. Time was passing, each second seeming to take an eternity as she twirled closer to the magical sounds.

"Come to me . . ."

She spun faster, closer . . .

"Healer!"

Storm's urgent voice broke through the dreamlike fog, pulling Emily to an abrupt stop. The creature in front of her reacted, too, its eyes narrowing and its mouth opening in a vicious snarl. Emily gasped as the world slid back into focus and she realized she was staring at a pale white skull and gaunt cheekbones. A ghoulish grin twisted under haunting, evil eyes full of malice. It was the nightmare face from the football game!

Emily screamed, the noise ripping out of her, shattering

the last few strands of the eerie melody. Stumbling backward, she nearly lost her balance.

There was a whoosh of cold, dank air and a deafening explosion of noise, like every note in the world played at once. Then she heard the more familiar sound of rushing feet.

Stormbringer was at her side in an instant.

"Healer! What is it?"

"What? Did you see the monster?" Ozzie came running behind Storm. "I knew it! I told you it had to be a basilisk! See, she's frozen in place! Now what are we going to do?"

Emily tried to speak, to reassure them that she was all right. "Eerp" was all she could manage.

Ozzie quickly clambered up her pant leg and hopped onto her shoulder, to peer into her face. "Uh-oh," he said. "Not a basilisk. Looks more like the work of a mind-muncher. Do you remember your *name?*" he shouted into her ear.

Emily winced and pushed him off her shoulder. "Stop that!" she said. "I'm not deaf. And of course I know my name."

"What did you see, healer?" Storm asked, concerned.

Emily glanced nervously toward the trees. But the spot where she'd seen the apparition was empty; only a few leaves and twigs hung there now. "It—it—I don't know," she stammered. "I mean, I think I saw—it was only there for a second."

She managed to point to the spot. Storm bounded over and circled the trees, carefully examining the ground with eyes, nose, and paws. *"There might have been something here, but it's gone now,"* she said after a moment.

Emily shook her head, trying to clear it of the lingering fog left by the monster's eerie music. She had seen this thing twice now, and she still didn't know what it was.

"Listen, you two," she began. "The thing I saw was—wait!"

A note rang in her ear, the faint hint of sound, clean and pure.

She slowly turned to a curtain of thick autumn leaves hanging between the trees. With Ozzie and Storm on each side, she carefully reached out and parted the curtain of colors.

Screeeeeeeeee!

Something large burst out of the woods straight at them, almost trampling Ozzie on its way. The explosion of sound was so sudden and overwhelming that Emily was knocked backward onto the ground. Off-key chords grated against one another, echoing through the woods and slicing into her head. Scrambling to her knees, she caught flashes of a horselike shape. It had a bright turquoise hide and a mane and tail that shimmered silvery blue. She pointed and shouted, though her words were lost in the cacophony of sound.

Storm was already after it.

"Storm! No! Wait!" Emily paused just long enough to scoop Ozzie up before following, running wildly through the woods. Ahead, the creature dove into a thick patch of brambles and disappeared.

"There!" Emily cried as the noise faded, leaving behind only faint, staticky reverberations. "It went that way!"

A flash of movement rattled the far side of the thicket. Then a patch of fuchsia caught the sun as a large shape crashed through the shadowy underbrush. A second later, Emily caught a glimpse of garish purple.

Storm started to run in that direction, but a huge, twisted shrub blocked her way. Panting, she darted around it. Emily shielded her face and followed.

"Ahh!" Ozzie shrieked, clinging to her for dear life. "Watch out for that branch!"

Emily ducked just in time to avoid getting smacked by a gnarled tree limb. Unfortunately she failed to notice the exposed root in her path. Her sneaker caught on it and she went flying, landing with a thud in a pile of dry autumn leaves.

"Whoooo-*aaaah!*" Ozzie flew off her shoulder and landed a few feet away. "Urfff!"

By the time they managed to sit up and make sure nothing was broken, Storm had returned. *"Whatever it is, it has powerful magic. I couldn't get near it,"* the mistwolf admitted, panting.

Ozzie nodded, brushing a twig out of his fur. "I think

it's safe to say we're not following a basilisk," he said. "My guess is pegasi."

Emily sat up, thinking back to the brief glimpse she'd caught of the creature. "I didn't see any wings. Why do you say 'it,' Storm? Seemed like several creatures."

"I could only make out one set of tracks," Storm answered.

"Are you suggesting it's *one* creature?" Ozzie asked. "They were all around us. How could one animal move so fast?"

Emily bit her lip. "One set of tracks," she said. "I could feel it—it's hurting bad," she whispered.

She looked up to see Storm sitting directly in front of her. They were almost nose to nose. The wolf's golden eyes glowed deep and warm.

"Perhaps you should open yourself to those feelings, try to follow them," the mistwolf suggested.

Emily looked at the ground. "I'm afraid."

"Fear is the worst enemy we face. I am here."

Emily knew the mistwolf was right, but she hesitated. She had just healed so many, felt so much fear and suffering. How much more did she have to give? Even Adriane and Kara didn't really know the toll it took on her.

Still, she had to reach inside and find the strength. It might be the only way to help the creature—or creatures—that clearly needed her help. "Okay," she said. "I'll try."

"Hang on to me."

Emily reached around the wolf's neck and hugged the animal close. Doing her best to keep her mind clear and still, she closed her eyes and breathed in deeply, exhaling in a whoosh.

Soft fur against her cheek, Emily smelled pine and forests, clean and sweet. She felt the strength of the wolf against her like a wall, impenetrable and solid.

The rainbow jewel flashed brightly, and she reached out with her mind.

The emotions hit her in a wallop, making her cry out in shock and pain. Instantly she felt Storm's iron will bolster her. *"Steady, healer."*

She stayed open, inviting the fierce pain, intense anger, and violent sorrow into her very soul. These feelings were stronger than those she had felt from the quiffles and jeeran back in the meadow. And a powerful undercurrent of magic throbbed along with these emotions, twisting them, making them stronger and more dangerous until Emily was gasping raggedly for breath.

"Don't run. I want to help," she said breathlessly. Her jewel glowed with an intense blaze of color. Then all was quiet.

Arms still wrapped tightly around Storm's neck, she opened her eyes. Ozzie was on her shoulder, arms wrapped tightly around her neck, his eyes shut, his ferret brow furrowed in intense concentration.

"You can let go now, Ozzie," Emily said, pulling away from Storm.

Ozzie's eyes flew open and he leaped back.

Emily gave each of her friends a kiss. "Thank you, both."

"No problem," Ozzie said proudly. "Did you get through?"

"I don't know." She got up and started into the forest. "This way."

Storm and Ozzie flanked her as she walked, following the trail of shifting emotions. Her rainbow stone gleamed steadily with dark, murky colors. Agony, dread, and desperation pulsed through her body, grabbing her heart and squeezing it, faster and faster, until it felt as though it would burst right out of her chest and—

"Wait." Storm's voice broke into her mind. *"Something is following us."*

At the sudden interruption, Emily's concentration faltered and the magical connection slipped. Her heart beating faster, she turned to see the mistwolf gazing intently at a dense copse of evergreens. The thick fur along Storm's spine was standing on end.

Ka-thunk. Ka-thunk.

The sounds of heavy feet pounded the earth, headed toward them.

Ozzie and Emily huddled close together. "What is it, Storm?" she asked.

Stormbringer bared her teeth and a low growl rumbled in her throat. *"Stay behind me, healer."* Her voice was grim. *"It comes."*

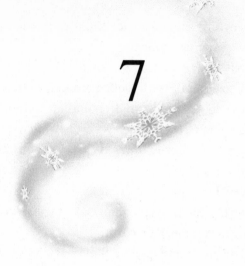

7

K A-THUNK. KA-THUNK.

The sound came directly toward them, flat steps falling with a dull thud. Storm and Ozzie moved in front of Emily. The wolf tensed, growling low. Ozzie grabbed a stick from the ground and held it up like a club. Nearby, leaves and branches rustled. Then the steps came to a halt.

Emily panicked, remembering that horrible, ghoulish face, those deep-socketed, soulless eyes. If that hideous specter stepped out of the trees, she would surely lose her mind. The branches parted.

A large, rotund creature hopped out.

Hopped? Emily raised her eyebrows in surprise. It looked a like a giant frog. It had lumpy blue-and-purple skin, flippers for feet, and a wide mouth stretched across its face in a perpetual smile.

"Look out!" the giant frog screamed.

Emily, Ozzie, and Storm looked around, confused.

"A mistwolf!" It whispered, pointing a flipper at Storm. It's bulbous, crystalline eyes were wide with fear.

"What the—" Ozzie lowered his weapon. Storm stopped growling.

"She won't hurt you," Emily explained.

"She won't?" The frog creature was not convinced.

"Not unless you mean us harm."

"Me?" The creature slapped a flipper against its chest.

Ozzie stomped up to it, examining it carefully. "It's a flobbin!" he exclaimed.

"A what?" Emily stared at the newcomer, who was easily as tall as she was but three times as wide.

A long, ribbonlike purple tongue flicked out over Ozzie's head.

"Gah!" The ferret frantically wiped his head with both front paws.

"I didn't think any animals from this world talked," the flobbin said.

"I'm special." Ozzie kicked the big frog. "And I am not edible!"

"Oh. Well, thank goodness I found you," the flobbin continued. "I've been wandering around for hours in these forests."

"Flobbins are fairy creatures," Storm explained to Emily. *"They are made mostly of fairy magic."*

"Is it dangerous?"

"Not that I know of."

"Dangerous? Heavens, no!" The flobbin took a hop closer to Emily but stepped back as Storm walked between them. "I was on assignment for the Fairimentals, looking for magic blobs."

"What's a magic blob?" Emily asked.

"You know, pockets of loose fairy magic. Some blobs are quite large and dangerous. I track the blobs, map them out, and report to the Fairimentals for proper handling."

"You know the Fairimentals?" Emily asked him.

"Sure." The flobbin shrugged his sloping, warty blue shoulders. "The F-sters and I go way back. Say, maybe you can help me. I'm supposed to find an elf called Ozymandias."

"*Gah!* That's me!" Ozzie jumped up and down.

"Really?" Big, bulbous eyes looked Ozzie over. "You're awfully fuzzy."

"It's a long story. Trust me."

"My name is Ghyll," the creature announced.

"I'm Emily, and this is Stormbringer." Emily waved her hand to include the wolf.

"I was heading to the Fairy Glen when everything went crazy," Ghyll explained, keeping a wary eye on the mistwolf. "The portals got all mixed up and I ended up here. At first I thought I was in the Moorgroves, near Dingly Dell."

"Dingly Dell?" Ozzie's eyes went wide.

"I have many elf friends there. Donafi, Brommy, Fernie—"

"Brommy's my cousin!" Ozzie cried delightedly.

"Yes, he's the one who told me about you."

"How is that rotten little pointy-eared creep?"

"Oh, he's fine," Ghyll said.

"Do you know what's happening on Aldenmor?" Emily interrupted.

"All portals to the Fairy Glen have been closed. It's as if the Fairy Glen just vanished."

"That's awful!" Ozzie exclaimed.

"So I guess I'm stuck here," Ghyll said.

"You and all the others that got through," Emily pointed out. "Are you hurt?"

"No."

"Well, if you need anything round these parts, I'm your elf," Ozzie said.

"I've been hopping around in these woods for hours and I'm famished. What do you have to eat in this world?" Ghyll's long purple tongue snapped out.

"Now you're talking my language!" Ozzie grinned and patted himself on the chest. "Stick with me. They have the most incredible food here, you won't believe it—"

"Er, Ozzie?" Emily broke in, knowing that the ferret could easily discuss food all day long. "Why don't you take Ghyll back and get him settled in? Storm and I can keep going without you."

"Where are you going?" Ghyll asked, blinking big eyes.

Emily hesitated only for a moment before answering. After all, if Storm and Ozzie felt the flobbin was a creature of good magic, she had nothing to worry about. "We think some injured creature ran away into the woods," she explained. "We're trying to track it down so we can help it."

"I'm a natural magic tracker. Perhaps I can help," Ghyll offered, puffing out his large chest.

Emily gave a quick glance at Storm, then asked Ghyll, "You haven't seen anything . . . peculiar around the woods, have you?"

Mistwolf, ferret, and flobbin looked at one another.

"That's a relative question," Ghyll answered.

"Come on, Ghyll!" Ozzie grabbed a flipper and pointed toward the trail. "I'll show you around Ravenswood."

"Excellent." Ghyll looked down at Ozzie. "Lead the way!"

Emily and Storm continued in the opposite direction. The sun angled on its late afternoon arc, sending bright patches gleaming off leaves and rocks.

"What do you make of Ghyll?" Emily asked Storm.

"I sensed nothing dangerous about the creature," the mistwolf answered.

"Something doesn't feel right. I mean, if he's a magic tracker for the Fairimentals as he says, he's not very good."

"How so?"

"There's enough wild magic flying around here to attract every creature on Aldenmor, and yet Ghyll didn't even mention he sensed any magic."

"He didn't say he didn't, either," Storm said.

"Yes, I suppose."

Emily turned her attention back to finding the hurt creature. She was afraid the encounter with Ghyll had wasted valuable time. How far had the magical creature gone?

"Why don't you try to reach out again?" Storm suggested.

Emily faltered. "Let's just check the clearing beyond those trees."

She pushed through the underbrush, Storm at her side. Suddenly she changed direction.

"This way," she said, heading across a small, nearly dry streambed. The signal had shifted; whatever they were following was still on the move.

But what *were* they following? All she knew was that something was out there, and she had to find it. An all-too-familiar grinning skull face popped into her head, but she refused to consider it. What they were after couldn't be evil.

Still, Emily felt frustrated. "How are we supposed to help creatures that won't even let us get close?"

Storm shook her shaggy gray head. *"If a creature is too far gone to recognize help when it comes, it may be too late."*

"No!" The word flew from Emily's mouth before she could stop it. "We can't give up. We have to keep going."

Storm gazed at her with patient golden eyes. *"Lead on, healer."*

A slight breeze carried a light note. Listening closely, Emily picked up a fast swirl of faint static, like interference on a car radio. Within the jumble, she caught a flurry of notes. They reminded her of the crazy noise that had emerged from her flute that morning.

Storm was looking at her. *"Healer, you are tired. Tomorrow is another day."*

All the energy seeped out of Emily. What was the point of continuing this ridiculous game? Storm was right. The creature didn't want to be found, and wandering around in the woods wasn't helping anyone. They might as well go home. She felt the familiar wall of despair closing in until she wasn't sure she could keep the tears at bay any longer.

She stopped suddenly. A wave of magic was building. Again! She felt it rushing towards her, sweeping through the trees, thundering past rocks and over streams. "Storm, run!" Emily yelled. But there was nowhere to go.

Storm howled, turning to face an enemy that wasn't there. With a rushing roar, the magic peaked, crashing down around them like a tidal wave breaking against a rocky shore.

Emily braced herself for pain—instead, she was swept away into a dream.

She twirled and spun through snowy, shimmering mists, listening to music. Wondrous deep sounds echoed, rising and falling in the vast space, each note reaching into the depths of her soul. The mists parted to reveal a path of stars, twinkling like diamonds under her feet. The music echoed over streams of pathways spread out before her, a million lights as far as her eyes could see.

Ahead, the path began to break apart, dissolving in great bursts of fire. Emily panicked. The fire raced toward her. Burning, searing agony attacked every inch of her body. Horrible fear and guilt ripped through her. Terror stole her breath and squeezed her heart like a vise.

Emily realized she was feeling the pain of the wounded creature. She couldn't give up. As the dark feelings swirled through her, Emily fought to keep herself open to them. She had to stay strong and focused. She could feel her rainbow stone pulsing warmly with the unsteady beat.

Something flew at her. She caught the hint of a blade, the flash of steel. Fast and vicious, it sliced toward her.

She screamed, and her eyes flew open. She was standing in the forest.

"Are you all right, healer?" Storm's voice in her head sounded worried.

Emily's breath came in ragged gulps. "I don't know," she croaked, plunging off the path at an angle, straight through a thick tangle of underbrush. She hardly noticed as vines grabbed at her hair and brambles pricked her skin.

She rushed through a cluster of trees and stopped at the edge of a meadow. Bending over to catch her breath, she curled her hands into fists and pounded the air in frustration. What's the point? Even if we find the creature, there's no guarantee I'll be able to help it. Emily was becoming exhausted. On the verge of tears, she swallowed hard and tried to remain calm. I might as well just turn around now and—

Wiping sweat-streaked hair from her face, she stared in amazement. There, standing across the clearing, was the most beautiful creature she'd ever seen.

8

*E*MILY HARDLY DARED to breathe, staring in awe at the creature. It looked like a delicately built mare. She stood about sixteen hands high and had a finely chiseled head and round, polished hooves. Her lavish mane and forelock were tangled and wild. In the reddish late-afternoon sunlight, the creature's coat looked magenta. She must have been wondrously beautiful before Black Fire had ravaged her colorful coat, leaving it charred and covered with patches of sickly green glow. She was trembling in fear.

"*Stand back, healer,*" Storm growled, stepping out of the brush, her hackles up.

The horse snorted at the mistwolf's appearance, her eyes rolling back in terror. Kicking up her rear hooves, she spun and leaped—and vanished. A burst of loud, angry, chaotic sound followed.

Emily was stunned.

"Wait!" she cried desperately. The creature couldn't run away again—not now that she'd finally seen her!

The horse suddenly reappeared at the far end of the clearing. She was gazing at Emily suspiciously, flanks heaving, breath coming in short, ragged bursts. Her coat was now a bright shade of reddish-yellow. Emily felt waves of fear emanate from the creature.

"Storm, she's afraid of you," Emily realized. "Stay in the woods for a minute. I'll call if I need you."

The mistwolf hesitated, then nodded. *"Be careful."* She melted back into the forest.

"It's okay," Emily whispered. She could feel pain and apprehension sweeping toward her. "I won't hurt you."

As she spoke, the creature's coat shifted to a shimmering pale aqua, then to a rusty orange, then to a swirl of deep blue, before paling again and changing to a radiant red. That was one mystery solved, Emily realized. They hadn't been following a herd of different-colored creatures after all—just one that changed color from moment to moment.

She stepped forward cautiously, her gaze fixed on the angry burns. The closer she got, the worse they looked. Her stomach churned. How had this wounded horse even survived this long?

"Easy," Emily murmured. The animal raised her head

and danced backward, her coat flashing reddish-purple. The healer forced herself to stand still and wait until the creature settled down again. "It's okay. I want to help."

The horse didn't run away, but she didn't come any closer, either. Emily bit her lip. Now what?

Patience. She heard her mother's voice inside her head. *Patience is the number one rule when you're dealing with animals. The number two and number three rules, too.*

Emily knew that. But it wasn't easy to stand there doing nothing when the creature in front of her was wracked with pain that only seemed to grow with every passing moment.

She told herself to remain calm. Freaking out wasn't going to help. The animal's gaze met her own, and in the soft greenish-gold eyes Emily could see the intense fear.

She took a step forward. The horse tensed and took a quick step back. Emily sighed and retreated. Then the animal stepped forward, gold-tipped ears pricked toward the girl.

"It's okay," Emily said, and the creature jumped in surprise.

This wasn't working. Emily decided to try communicating in a different way.

She tried to fill her mind with soothing images. *"I'm your friend. I want to help you."*

The animal cocked her head, staring at Emily suspiciously. There was a sudden blare of that jarring noise and a jumble of feelings.

Emily waited. Her hands were twitching, wanting to touch the animal and try to heal her wounds. But she knew that wouldn't happen unless she could win her trust.

Pain. Fear and pain. Notes, emerging suddenly out of the white noise.

Emily listened. Was that—?

She shook her head. She had to be imagining things, didn't she? She couldn't possibly be hearing what she thought she'd just heard.

Without quite knowing why, she hummed the first few notes of "her" song.

The horse stood stock-still and raised her head, and for a moment Emily was afraid she'd scared her again. Then the confusion of noise in her head cleared for a second—and echoed the same notes back to her!

Emily gasped. "You heard me!" she exclaimed out loud. "You understood!"

The horse repeated the first few notes—all at once—but the tune got lost in the chaos of white noise and jangled chords. Then she lowered her graceful head and let out a low, sad whine.

Emily pointed to herself. "I'm Emily."

She focused her thoughts again. *"What's your name?"* she asked.

Another burst of static. Then—a single word.

"Lorelei." The voice coming from the animal's mind was feminine and musical-sounding.

"Lorelei," Emily whispered. Was that her name or the name of a kind of creature, like a quiffle or a flobbin? She had no way of knowing, but somehow she was certain that it was the former. So then what *was* Lorelei?

She shook that question away. The important thing now was to stay connected so she could get close enough to heal Lorelei's wounds.

Taking another step forward, Emily held her breath. The creature gazed at her. Fluctuating, uncertain feelings flashed in the greenish-gold eyes—doubt, suspicion, worry—but Emily kept her own gaze steady.

Patience. Patience. Let her feel your good intentions, she told herself.

The creature stared back. A few notes danced through Emily's head, and she felt a shock go through her, like being struck by lightning. Through the shock she was aware that a connection had been made, a bond that was almost frightening in its intensity. What it meant, she didn't know.

She wasn't sure how much longer it was before she took another step forward, and another. Each time, she stopped the moment she sensed Lorelei tensing up and preparing to retreat. Each time, she waited for the animal's eyes to calm before moving again.

Finally, they were standing only two feet apart. "All right," Emily murmured, trying not to look at the angry burns that seemed to swallow up her body. "Now it's up to you, Lorelei."

For several long, breathless moments, nothing happened. Girl and magic horse stood and stared at each other. The only thing that changed was the rainbow jewel at Emily's wrist, which cycled steadily—blue, gold, scarlet, indigo.

Emily waited. She could feel herself aching with the agonizing burn of the Black Fire. It was hard to stand there and look at the terrible wounds—hard to stand there and not rush to help. But somehow she knew there was no other way. Finally, Lorelei trembled and took a small, cautious step forward.

That was enough. Emily slowly reached forward and touched the animal on the shoulder . . .

Instantly, the forest tilted at a crazy angle and dropped away. And she heard it again, that dreadful noise blaring, screaming, frantic—the gleaming edge of steel flashed, cutting through flesh and bone.

Emily cried out and tried to pull her hand away. But she couldn't move. *Focus! Focus!*

Squeezing her eyes shut, she tried to make sense of what she was doing. She had to concentrate on the healing. That's why she was here.

Then one tone leaped out at her, and she locked onto it. A note. One pure note in the pandemonium. It came again, deep and resonant. Her own heartbeat. It slowed and steadied as she suddenly became aware of another heartbeat matching her own, pulsing raggedly but strongly. An image of Lorelei danced in front of her, her

wounded coat bathed in a swirling white light, familiar and yet—what was it? What was different about her? Emily shuddered as her focus wavered . . .

The Black Fire was stronger than she had ever encountered before. Was Emily strong enough to fight it? She didn't dare think about it. Instead, she focused on the matched heartbeats and on the melody that rose up to mingle and harmonize with them, growing louder and stronger with each beat. It was a familiar melody and Emily found herself listening eagerly, aching to hear the last few notes that would make the song complete.

"What are you?" Emily asked.

Images of a pristine snowfall drifted into Emily's mind.

"I don't understand." She tried to reach deeper.

A family—mother, father, and three little ones—running, racing strong and sure along a golden thread of stars. Each of the creatures had a crystalline horn at the center of their foreheads. Sparkling trails of magic spiraled into looping patterns and the music they made was heart-wrenching in its beauty.

Emily was awed.

The image burst apart with a blare of harsh, staticky noise. The wild sound picked her up and she was carried forward, her heart racing crazily and her lungs gasping for breath.

"No!" she cried desperately. She felt the connection rupture, and her eyes flew open. Lorelei was springing away, her eyes wide and rolling with fright. "Wait!" But it was too late. The creature leaped into the air and vanished.

"Healer!"

Storm's urgent voice exploded inside her head, and Emily whirled around to see the mistwolf racing toward her, lips drawn back in a threatening snarl.

"No!" Emily cried, falling to her knees. She felt overwhelmed by despair—she had come so close, only to be wrenched back at the wrong moment. "Storm, no!"

Stormbringer skidded to a stop in front of her and let out a low growl. *"Did you not sense the danger?"*

Emily blinked, not sure at first what the mistwolf was talking about. Then she glanced around.

The ground was littered with branches, leaves, and other debris. Several large boulders were scattered about like a giant's game of billiards. Furrows of fresh dirt crisscrossed the clearing, like gashes in the earth itself. An enormous, ancient oak tree had been ripped up by its roots and lay at a crazy angle across the clearing—one huge bough only a few feet from the spot where Emily was crouched.

"Wha—when did this happen?" she gasped.

Storm was gazing at her intently. *"When the two of you connected."* She didn't bother to finish, merely shaking her shaggy head and glancing around at the destruction in the clearing.

Emily buried her face in her hands. What was

happening? She thought she had made a connection with Lorelei. But at the last moment, the creature had given up, run away. Why? She shuddered as she remembered the hopelessness and fear and something else—shame.

The last image floated back into her mind, full-formed and clear. She looked up, her eyes widening as she realized for the first time what had been different about the creature.

"Storm," she breathed. "I think I know what she is. Lorelei. She's a—a unicorn!"

EMILY WALKED INTO the circular driveway in front of Ravenswood Manor. The grand building was more than a century old. When Emily had first seen it, she had been spooked by the strange Gothic manor, complete with gargoyles perched on stone parapets. Now she welcomed the strength of its solid stone and seasoned wood. The big front windows watched her, looking down in welcome.

So many other things seemed so fleeting, she mused. How something so real, so close, could vanish in an instant, gone in the blink of an eye.

Emily blew out a frustrated sigh and shifted her backpack to her other shoulder. She followed the cobblestone walkway around the manor and entered the first of many gardens that surrounded the great lawns. Her friends were probably already in the portal field. They had planned to meet there and discuss what to do about the portal. Somehow they had to figure out how to replace the dreamcatcher that had protected it from evil.

"Emily?"

Adriane's grandmother was working in one of the rose gardens. Nakoda—better known to Adriane and her friends as Gran—was the caretaker of Ravenswood. She had worked for its owner, Mr. Gardener, for many years before Adriane had come to live with her.

"Oh," Emily muttered. "Hi." Lowering her head to avoid the woman's wise, observant gaze, she started to hurry past. She just wasn't in the mood for dealing with adults right now. *Any* adults.

The old woman clipped several magnificent yellow and red roses, carefully settling them in her bag, then held up her pruning shears. "Nurturing, care, and love."

"Huh?"

"To flourish and blossom, it takes more than peat moss and plant food."

"Yeah."

"What's the matter, dear?" Gran asked. "Your face is as dark as a thundercloud."

"Sorry," Emily snapped without thinking. "I didn't know that being in a good mood was a requirement for coming here."

She immediately regretted the sharp words. Her face flushed with shame, and she stared at her feet. But Gran hardly seemed to notice as she stood up.

"Come," she said. "Walk with me."

Emily sighed and walked beside Gran across the great lawn toward the maze of gardens. Gran took a deep breath, looking around. "The world is full of colors today, isn't it?"

"Sure." Emily glanced around, too, suddenly noticing the brilliant, ever-changing autumn colors of the maples and the oaks, the dogwoods and the sweet gums.

Gran was watching her. "It's amazing what one sees

when one's eyes are open," she commented. "What good is a rainbow if we only focus on one color?"

"Gran," Emily began hesitantly. "Do you think someone who's injured has to *want* to get better?"

Gran nodded soberly. "If the spirit does not desire healing, no true healing can take place, even if the body seems to recover."

"But why would a person or animal just give up when there's still hope?" Emily pressed on. "Especially if there are people trying to help?"

"Hope means different things to different people," Gran replied. "And if you want to help, you have to be willing to give the kind of help that's needed, not just the kind you *think* is needed."

Emily wasn't quite sure what the old woman meant. After all, her mother didn't ask each dog what it needed before she treated it.

Gran must have seen the confusion in her eyes. "Think of it this way," she said, leaning over to pick up a stick from the ground. "The physical and the spiritual often intersect. Like this." She scratched a figure in the dirt—one strong line going up and down, another crossing it from side to side. "Sometimes there is suffering on the physical line only, or on the spiritual line only. But when the pain lies right here"—she pointed with the stick to the spot where the lines bisected—"that is when healing can be most difficult."

"Oh." Emily nodded, thinking of Lorelei. The

unicorn—or whatever she was—had been badly injured by the Black Fire on the outside. What if she had been just as badly injured on the inside? "But how can you help someone like that?"

Gran shrugged, dropping the stick on the ground. "By remaining open to all possibilities. If one way isn't working, try another. And another. And another after that, if necessary."

"But what if you run out of ways?"

Gran shook her head firmly. "There are infinite possibilities in this world," she said, "just as there are infinite shades within a rainbow. It's just a matter of opening your heart to them."

Emily chewed on her lower lip. "I guess," she said hesitantly.

Gran smiled. "Emily," she said, "you can never truly fail as long as you give all of yourself to the attempt."

Emily watched the autumn colors dance through the forests, a bold display before winter's gray grip took hold. Why was it her burden to feel so much pain and loss? How was she supposed to handle it? It took only one image of the wounded Lorelei in her mind to bolster her resolve. She was a healer and one thing she could never do was give up, no matter how difficult things may seem. She took a deep breath and braced herself for what lay ahead.

10

"*T*HIS ISN'T GOING to work."

"Okay, guys, do your thing! Go ahead! You can do it!"

Zzzzzinnnng! Pop! Buzzzzz! Slllllurrrrp!

"No! No! You're not supposed to *eat* the spaghetti, you goofballs!"

"Yummmmmyyyyyyyyyy!"

"Aargh! Stop them, Kara! I have noodles in my hair!"

Even before Emily entered the meadow, she could hear the loud, excited voices drifting toward her on the slight breeze. What in the world was going on?

She stepped into the field just in time to see Adriane brushing frantically at her long, dark hair as Stormbringer circled her anxiously. Lyra was crouching in the grass, batting at Fred as the dragonfly flew about, skillfully missing the big cat's playful swipes. Nearby, the other dragonflies, Barney, Goldie, Blaze, and Fiona, and others Kara had not named, careened around the field, leaving trails of twinkly magic sparks everywhere. Kara was waving her arms around, obviously trying to control the cluster of dragonflies.

"Emmpheee!" Goldie flitted toward Emily, banking just in front of her face.

"Hello, Goldie. What have you got there?"

"Magiccc noodilll!" Goldie squeaked.

Adriane glanced at her and rolled her eyes. "We're testing another one of Miss America's lame-brained ideas," she replied.

"I don't see you coming up with anything better, Miss Crouching Tiger," Kara snapped back.

Emily held her hands up to avoid getting hit with a wet noodle. "Whoa," she said. "Somebody fill me in, okay?"

"Since the dragonflies wove the last dreamcatcher, I figured they could weave another one," Kara explained. "I even let them take a few strands of my hair, and that didn't work." She crossed her arms over her chest, then ducked as Blaze buzzed past, wobbling crazily under a mass of spaghetti strands.

Emily had to admit that the plan made some sense but, "Spaghetti?"

"I like spaghetti. It could work," Kara said.

A few weeks ago, a wild burst of uncontrolled magic

had caused Kara's hair to grow super long and turn every color of the rainbow. Once her hair had been trimmed, the dragonflies had used the cut strands to weave a protective web over the portal. It had worked like a dreamcatcher, only instead of keeping nightmares away it had covered the portal to keep nightmare *creatures* from coming through. That way, only good magical creatures had been able to pass through when the portal opened. But now the dreamcatcher was gone.

Emily glanced at Adriane.

The dark-haired girl grimaced. "We've already tried Kara's yarn, some ribbon, some socks, and now this."

"Yeah," Kara added morosely. "That spaghetti was supposed to be lunch today."

"Well, there's always more possibilities, right?" Emily said, remembering what Gran had just told her. "We just need to find something else with Kara's magic touch to give them."

Adriane stared thoughtfully at Lyra. "Hmm," she said. "What about—"

Poooowieeee!" Fred went flying as Lyra batted him across the field.

"*I don't think so,*" the cat interrupted before Adriane could finish, backing away warily.

Emily brushed away Blaze, who was buzzing excitedly near her left shoulder, and pointed at Kara's feet. "What about those?"

Kara looked down at her pink sneakers. "You mean my

shoelaces?" she exclaimed. "I had to search every store in the mall to find these! They exactly match my pink base-ball cap."

"Fashion is so fickle, you know," Adriane commented. "I heard purple is the new pink."

"All you ever wear is black, so how would you know?" Kara rolled her eyes, but took off her sneakers. As she slid the laces out of the holes, she glanced at Emily. "Hey," she said. "What's happening with our mystery guest?"

"Pretty much what I already told you," Emily sighed. She'd emailed Kara and Adriane about Lorelei as soon as she'd gotten home last night. "I just can't seem to get through to her. How are all the new animals?" she asked instead.

"Fine. Most of them are over at the glade. Ozzie and some of the others are filling them in on this world and everything," Adriane told her.

Pink shoelaces in hand, Kara said, "Storm doesn't think Lorelei is a unicorn. And neither do I."

"Why not?"

"Think about it." Kara tapped herself on the forehead. "What do unicorns have that makes them so special? Duh. A *horn*."

"Yes, you're right, but still . . ."

Kara waggled her shoelaces in the air. "Yoo-hoo, guys," she called to the dragonflies. "I've got something else for you to play with."

The dragonflies buzzed over and eagerly grabbed the

shoelaces, spinning them into small webs. Tiny, colorful sparks started to pop in the air all around them.

"This is nuts. The dreamcatcher has to be made from something stronger, some real magic!" Adriane said.

"We're waiting for your suggestions, Snow Black," Kara quipped.

Ignoring Kara, Adriane went on. "We know something has happened in Aldenmor and it most likely involves the Dark Sorceress. We need to think of something more effective to cover the portal if it opens again."

Emily bit her lip. She understood why her friends were so focused on fixing the dreamcatcher. As long as the portal remained unprotected, there was no telling what might come through when it opened again. But she couldn't seem to concentrate. Not while Lorelei was still out there somewhere in the woods, alone and scared.

"I'm going back out," she said as casually as she could. "See if I can find Lorelei again."

The other girls exchanged a glance. "I'm not sure that's such a good idea," Adriane said.

"She's right," Kara agreed. "It sounds like that non-unicorn of yours is pretty dangerous. What if it's the evil something Zach warned us about?"

"Evil?" Emily echoed in surprise. "Lorelei isn't evil."

Adriane ducked as two dragonflies swooped past, inches from her head, furiously trying to spin tiny pink dreamcatchers. "Well, knocking down trees and throwing around boulders doesn't exactly sound good to me."

"Lorelei didn't mean to do all that." Emily couldn't believe how her friends were reacting. They hadn't even been there! She whirled toward the mistwolf. "Storm, tell them!"

Storm met her gaze steadily. *"The creature has very strong magic,"* she said. *"So strong that she seems unable to control it. That counts as dangerous."*

Glancing over her shoulder, Emily saw Ghyll hopping over to them. Ozzie was strolling next to the flobbin.

"Hey, Ozzie," Kara said, staring curiously at the giant froglike creature. "Who's your new friend?"

Emily realized that Kara must not have seen Ghyll the day before. She was about to explain.

But before she could say a word, Ghyll suddenly straightened up, his bulging eyes seeming to expand to twice their usual size. His warty blue skin glowed as his mouth opened in astonishment, purple tongue rolling onto the ground. "Well, hello there!" he cried out, leaping forward so eagerly Ozzie went flying.

"Hey!" the ferret cried. "Watch it!"

Ghyll didn't even seem to hear him. His gaze was pinned on Kara. He hopped up to her and stopped. "Most beautiful of creatures," he said breathlessly. "I am Ghyll, your most humble and adoring servant."

"Hey. Not so close." Kara brushed her blond hair back from her face, dislodging a stray spaghetti noodle as she did so. "I'm Kara Davies, *the* most beautiful of creatures."

"What ravishing beauty!" Ghyll hopped closer still, gazing at Kara adoringly. "Would you honor me with a kiss?"

Kara wrinkled her nose. "I don't think so," she said, taking a step backward. "I'm on a break."

Ghyll leaned forward eagerly. His bulging eyes were level with Kara's forehead. "Just one little kiss—to turn me into a handsome prince!"

He puckered his wide, rubbery lips and closed his eyes. Lyra stood up, her fur bristling, pushing her way between the flobbin and the girl.

"She said no," the cat growled.

Lyra jumped as Ghyll planted a slobbery kiss right between her eyes. *"Bleeccch!"*

"Hey!" The flobbin's eyes flew open. "What's the big idea?"

Ozzie rolled on the ground, laughing. Even Storm looked amused.

"Is this frog for real?" Kara asked.

"He's a flobbin," Ozzie explained.

"Listen up, flubber, you've been reading too many fairy tales," Kara said. "I don't do magic kisses."

Kara took a few steps away from Ghyll as Lyra glared at the flobbin suspiciously. "Maybe the unicorn is a flipper, too—"

"Unicorn?" Ghyll broke in. "Is there a unicorn here?"

"No," Kara and Adriane replied at the same time Emily said, "Yes. Maybe."

"There is a magical creature on the loose," Storm explained to the flobbin. *"Horselike, but with no horn."*

"Ah." Ghyll blinked his bulbous eyes. "No horn means

no unicorn, right? It's probably an eqqtar—a wild Aldenmor pony." He glanced at Emily. "You should be careful," he added. "Eqqtari can be unpredictable at the best of times. And if this one's *pretending* to be a unicorn, well, who knows what it could be up to? You really ought to stay away from it. Far away."

Emily was about to respond when five despondent dragonflies plopped to the ground at her feet. "Uh-oh," she said, bending to pick up Barney. "I guess the shoelace thing isn't working either, huh?"

The dragonflies squeaked helplessly, sparks shooting out in all directions, and popped out of sight.

Adriane turned to Kara. "So what do we try next?"

Kara glanced at her pink-strapped watch. "Nothing, for now," she said. "We have a tour in, like, ten minutes." As part of their agreement with the town council, the girls had agreed to lead public tours of the Ravenswood Preserve on the weekends. Tourists could see exotic animals, just not the magical ones.

"I will come, too," Ghyll said eagerly. "I want to help you, beautiful princess of Earth. I will earn your love and gratitude."

"Fine," Kara said. "Go stand over there and hide." She pointed to a spot all the way across the field. "Forever."

"Your wish is my command!" Ghyll hopped away quickly.

Ozzie shook his head. "I'll make sure he stays out of the way," he murmured, scurrying after Ghyll.

"You guys probably don't need me for the tour, right?" Emily said to the other girls.

Adriane and Kara stared at her.

Emily shrugged stubbornly. "Whatever Lorelei is, she needs help. I'm not just going to abandon her."

"Just be careful," Adriane said.

"Okay."

"Storm and Lyra will check on you once the tour's finished."

Emily nodded as Kara and Adriane hurried toward the path leading back to the manor.

Soon the field was empty except for Emily. She bent over to pick up her backpack. The top flap was half open, and she noticed something sticking out. Huh?

She reached in and pulled out her flute. How had that gotten in there? She had taken it out to practice for the band tryout, but she always put it back in its case when she was done. Didn't she? She must have stuck it in her backpack without thinking.

"Oh well," she muttered aloud. She slung the backpack over her shoulder and walked into the woods, holding the flute in her hand. The smooth, cool metal felt somehow comforting, reassuring.

An hour later she stood at a crossroads in the trail, feeling stupid. What was she doing? She couldn't even *find* Lorelei, let alone help her. Meanwhile, her friends were stuck doing her share of things—not just the easy things, like leading tours of Ravenswood, but really important things, like trying to replace the dreamcatcher.

Glancing down at her jewel, she saw that it was cold and dark. If she didn't know better, she would think it was just a pretty hunk of lifeless rock.

Still, she kept walking.

Somewhere nearby, a twig cracked loudly. Emily glanced toward the sound.

And there was Lorelei just ahead of her, coat swirling with colors that changed so fast Emily couldn't keep track.

Emily gasped. "I—I thought you wouldn't come," she blurted.

The creature jumped, startled by her voice. Backing away, she gazed at Emily suspiciously.

"No, wait!" Emily had an idea. Putting the flute to her lips, she played a few bars of her song. Lorelei cocked her head, her expression wavering between interest and wariness.

Emily kept playing. A moment later, a humming sound filled the air around her. She tensed, expecting it to explode into that horrible, jarring noise she had heard before. But this time Lorelei's "singing" was clear and pure, her sweet voice wrapping around Emily's notes and carrying them, expanding them into something perfect and whole and—magical.

Lorelei approached Emily and knelt down before her. Holding her breath, Emily slowly lowered the flute. She moved close, hand outstretched and touched Lorelei's

head, combing through the silky mane with her fingers. Lorelei closed her eyes. Emily ran her hand down the creature's neck and back up over her head—and stopped. There was a small nub, like a slightly protruding bone, in the middle of Lorelei's forehead.

"What's this?" Emily asked, feeling the bump. Lorelei crooned softly.

Images flooded Emily's mind. Twinkling stars, spread out in a pattern, like a city seen from a nighttime flight. Circles of light, steady and beautiful.

Emily tried to send a few images of her own. Questions. What was she seeing? What was Lorelei trying to tell her? What had happened to her?

Lorelei's music grew hurried, almost frantic. The sounds were becoming different, darker. Anguished. Almost violent—

Crash!

A giant tree branch fell to the ground at Emily's feet. Startled, she jumped back, swinging her flute through the air—

A glint of steel, a horrible blade cutting into bone—

Lorelei's voice erupted into a jumble of screeching, painful noise. She reared up, looking at Emily, eyes wide in terror.

"Wait!" Emily gasped. "It was an accident. Don't go!"

Too late. With one last burst of noise, Lorelei vanished.

11

"*O*VER HERE! HE totally looked at me. He's just the cutest guy on the entire football team. I should so play 'We Will Rock You,' that's the first song I learned on flute. I'm going to do that for my solo, don't you think?"

Emily sighed, not bothering to answer. She knew the girl next to her wouldn't even notice. The band audition had been easy, since Emily could read music and had her own flute. That was about it. And now here she was, actually at the afternoon football game against Evanston High, sitting next to a chatterbox named Rae.

Slumping in her seat, she rested her chin on her hand and glanced out at the football field, where the players from both teams were huddling. What had possessed her to join the band anyway? It was just one more thing keeping her away from Ravenswood—and Lorelei. Not to mention her chores at the Pet Palace.

Thinking about the fight with her mother, she got a sick feeling in the pit of her stomach. When she'd arrived home last night, her mother had acted as if nothing had happened, and Emily had not brought it up, either. The two had pretty much avoided each other as much as possible all evening. This morning, Carolyn had left for the clinic by the time Emily had come down to breakfast.

Maybe that's the best way, she thought uncertainly. We should both just forget about what happened.

Pop!

Emily jumped, startled by the sound. She looked around frantically for any unidentified flying dragonflies.

Rae was staring at her from behind a huge bubble. She sucked it back into her mouth, then popped her gum noisily.

"Ravenswood has been there, like, forever," Rae chattered away. "Kinda too bad it'll all be gone soon."

"Ravenswood isn't going anywhere," Emily said firmly.

"My aunt says it's practically a done deal," Rae said in her loud, slightly nasal voice.

"Your aunt?" Turning to look directly at the other girl for the first time, Emily narrowed her eyes suspiciously.

Rae gazed back. The crisp autumn breeze lifted a loose strand of brown hair and blew it across her cheek. For the first time, Emily noticed that the other girl's face looked strangely familiar. Who else had those beady eyes, those broad, flat cheekbones, and that pointed nose?

"My Aunt Bea. She's right over there."

Emily looked where Rae was pointing. Mrs. Windor was sitting in the wooden bleachers directly across from the band, her thin frame wedged firmly between Mayor Davies and his wife.

"Mrs. Windor is your aunt?" Emily asked through clenched teeth.

"Uh-huh." Rae didn't even seem to notice Emily's dismay. "Aunt Bea told my mom a golf course is just what Stonehill needs, not an animal preserve." Leaning into Emily, she whispered, "You know the animals there are dangerous."

Emily knew that she should just ignore Rae. She knew all too well what Mrs. Windor thought about Ravenswood. Still, she felt anger bubbling up from deep inside her, hot and frantic. How dare Mrs. Windor decide what was best for the town? How dare she try to undo all their hard work, belittle Ravenswood's long history, and displace all those innocent animals?

Her gaze wandered to the field again, searching for the cheerleaders. Kara was standing in formation with the rest of the squad, watching the play on the field. Just behind the cheerleaders, Emily spotted Molly, Heather, and Tiffany. Sitting near them, but obviously not *with* them, was an unhappy-looking Adriane. Emily felt bad. She knew Adriane hated these school games. She shouldn't have asked Adriane to come hear her play. But Adriane *was* here, and Emily wondered if she should try to send her a magical message about what Rae had just said.

No, better not, she decided a second later. With the way my luck is going lately, I'd probably mess it up and cause another magical explosion or something. After what happened at the last game . . .

A soft, insistent burst of music startled her. For a second she thought she had missed a signal, that the band director had started a song without her knowing it, and she grabbed her flute. But then she realized that nobody else was playing, either.

Then where was that music coming from? She half closed her eyes, listening intently as the melody wrapped its way around her brain. How could music like that exist? So mysterious, so strange, and yet so familiar.

Her head started to feel fuzzy. Rae's voice faded until it was little more than an annoying drone at the heart of the silky melody. Glancing down at the field, Emily noted with surprise that the players seemed to be running in slow motion. The scene tilted, making her dizzy, and she grabbed at the hard bleacher seat to check her balance.

Wow, she thought. That's weird.

The only thing that wasn't moving in slow motion was her heart. It started to beat faster and faster. Her brain struggled to catch up.

This . . . has . . . happened . . . before, she thought. The music kept distracting her, confusing her, but somehow, somewhere at edge of her memory, she knew that something was about to happen. She could feel small eddies of magic swirling in the distance, building into a wave.

Oh, no! She tensed. Not again.

The rainbow jewel was throbbing at her wrist, its colors muddy green, sour yellow and blood-red.

Something was about to happen. Something bad.

Glancing around for help, she noticed the band director's shiny, bald head, which seemed somehow comforting all of a sudden. She forced herself to focus on it. If she just watched that, all this weirdness would go away.

The band director stood up. Lifting his baton, he turned around . . .

. . . and grinned directly at Emily with yellowish, crooked teeth. Gaping eye sockets leered at her, burning in dead white skin.

Emily opened her mouth to scream, but no sound came out. A nudge to her ribs made her turn.

"Come on, we're on," Rea whispered, already holding her flute to her lips.

Emily turned back to see the director's baton moving up and down, his normal, pudgy face concentrating on the trombone section.

Just breathe! she told herself.

Raising her instrument, Emily stared desperately toward her friends. Kara and the other cheerleaders were doing a routine, standing in a line and shaking their gold-and-blue pompoms over their heads, then down by their waists. As they lowered the pompoms, Emily looked for Adriane behind them. Her eyes scanned the crowd and stopped suddenly. There it was again. One horrible face—a gaunt, gruesome figure with dark evil eyes.

She jumped to her feet, her heart pounding so hard it seemed it would burst out of her chest.

"Hey, what are you doing?"

Rae's voice sounded faraway and weak. Ignoring her, Emily stood on her tiptoes, trying to see over the cheerleaders' waving pompoms. The hideous monster was just a few rows behind Adriane and the others. Was it after her friends? She had to warn them! Emily's arms felt leaden as she tried to wave back and forth.

Was it her imagination, or was the monster one row closer now? Its sly, menacing gaze was waiting to meet her own; it locked in on her—and nodded.

With immense effort, Emily managed to rip her gaze away. Taking a deep breath, she did her best to shake off the spell of the sinister music. She had to get a message to Adriane and Kara!

But trying to organize herself—focus her magic—was like wading through quicksand. The wheedling, mysterious music was pulling her deeper and deeper, and before long the struggle just didn't seem worth the effort. The ghoulish face had melted into the crowd, indistinguishable in the sea of faces. Emily felt heat at her wrist. She knew her jewel was pulsing a warning, but she didn't care. She sat down, listlessly holding her flute. Wherever she was being pulled, she should just give in, let it carry her wherever it would—even into the comfortable numbness of utter darkness.

Suddenly a clear, high note cut through the fog in her mind, followed by another. The crisp notes called to her. Emily sat up straight, almost dropping her flute.

All at once, the heavy, foggy feeling disappeared. The mysterious music had stopped, and Emily felt things snap into normal speed again.

And this time, she wasn't the only one reacting. All around her, people were murmuring and calling to each other.

"What is that?"

"Hey, check it out—down there on the field!"

"Is that a horse? What's it doing here?"

A flurry of notes rang out, cascading over Emily like delicate flakes of snow.

She glanced at her jewel, which was now pulsing with bright, clear light. Still clutching her flute, she pushed past Rae.

"Hey!" the other girl protested. "Where are you going?"

Emily ignored her. "Excuse me," she muttered, pushing her way forward. "Excuse me. I have to get through."

A chubby kid holding a trombone blocked her way. "Look at that thing! It's wild!" he said.

The call came again, frightened and panicked. Finally, one of the tall kids in front moved aside, and Emily had a clear view of the field at last. "Oh, no!" she breathed, astonished at what she saw.

It was Lorelei. At least she thought it was Lorelei. The creature stood at the edge of the field, near the visiting team's goal post. Now, her coat was a dazzling, snowy white instead of a multitude of shifting colors. Her silvery hooves gleamed in the sunlight, and her mane and tail were pure white silken strands.

But Emily hardly noticed any of that. She was staring at Lorelei's head, where a long, graceful spiral of a crystalline horn jutted proudly from her forehead.

"I knew it!" Emily whispered in awe. "You *are* a unicorn."

The unicorn shifted her head, long silky mane flowing, and looked around at the crowd, searching.

"I'm here," Emily whispered.

"Whoa!" one of the trumpet players cried. "What's it doing now?"

"I don't know, but looks like Coach Berman is going to kick its horsie butt!" another boy shouted. "Woot! Go Coach!"

Both teams' coaches and a dozen players were now running down the field toward the unicorn.

"No! Don't hurt her!" Emily yelled. She pushed her way to the playing field. The band members all turned to look at her.

"What's with her?" a sax player asked.

"Kara, Adriane!" Emily called.

Lorelei pawed at the ground, turning in a tight circle as more people surrounded her.

A flash of dark hair pushed through the crowd. Adriane stood face-to-face with three football players, yelling something and forcing them back. She was clearing a path for the unicorn to escape.

Lorelei was frantically looking left and right.

"Run!" Emily called.

The unicorn looked across the field to Emily, reared up, and raced through the break between the players.

"Hey, horsie! Stonehill can't win even *with* you!" A large bird stood in Lorelei's path, waving its arms up and down.

"Go, chicken guy!" Kids cheered from the bleachers.

"I am the Evanston Eagle!" the chicken guy announced, bowing to the stands.

The student dressed as the Evanston High Eagle wore an enormous round papier-mâché eagle's head. He moved toward Lorelei, dancing and flapping his arms, which were encased in fake wings lined with scraggly feathers that fluttered in the light breeze.

"Go, Evanston Eagle!" the visiting students cheered on their mascot as the chicken guy did his chicken dance.

Stonehill students booed. "Go, Stonehill Unicorn!" they chanted.

Lorelei snorted and fixed her large, liquid eyes on the

humans as they came up behind her. The chicken guy closed in, flapping its wings, "Evanston rules! For I am the chick—I mean, eagle!"

Chicken guy danced toward Lorelei, taunting her and trying to press her back towards the waiting players.

Lorelei reared up on her hind legs, and for a moment Emily thought she was going to wheel and vanish as she'd done before.

"No! No magic, *please!*" Emily breathed.

Lorelei landed with a snort, lowered her head . . .

. . . and charged.

"Nice horsie." Then a muffled scream came from inside the giant eagle head. "Ahhh!"

Chicken guy turned to run, but it was too late. Emily gasped and covered her eyes as Lorelei's gleaming horn ripped through the garish yellow beak and pierced the bulbous head.

When she peeked out through her fingers a second later, she saw Lorelei dancing in place, shaking her head frantically, trying to free herself from the giant hollow orb impaled on her horn. The kid in the mascot costume—minus the eagle's head—was running in the other direction. His hair was a little messy and his face a little pale, but otherwise he looked okay.

The crowd cheered. "Go, Stonehill!"

Suddenly an undercurrent of noisy, confused sound slammed into Emily. She almost screamed.

As waves of emotional magic rolled over her, nearly

buckling her knees, she could feel Lorelei's panic rising. Emily herself felt on the verge of hysteria. She had to get Lorelei out of there—now!

"Lorelei!" Emily pushed and shoved through the crowd, barreling out onto the sidelines. Lorelei had managed to free herself from the eagle's head at last. She was standing in the end zone, snorting at the cheering crowd. Adriane was trying desperately to hold back several big players, but it was only a matter of seconds before Lorelei would be trapped. Why doesn't she run?

Lorelei spun around, looking at Emily, waiting for her.

"Go! Run!" Emily yelled, taking a step onto the field.

A hand landed on her shoulder.

"This is the final straw, young lady!"

Emily whirled to find a wagging finger in her face. "Your animals are finished, and so is Ravenswood!" Mrs. Windor said.

"Let me go!" Emily yelled. Pulling away, she turned and sprinted across the field to Kara's side.

"Stand back, everyone," Kara said to the crowd, allowing Emily to get through. "We're professional tour guides!"

Lorelei stood, nodding her head toward Emily.

"Get her out of here! Now!" Kara whispered.

"I need some time," Emily said, moving slowly toward the terrified unicorn.

Kara saw Mrs. Windor grabbing some teachers and pointing at the girls. Even from here, she could tell Mrs.

Windor's face was flushed with anger as the woman started across the field. "Here comes trouble," Kara said.

She clapped her hands, grabbed her pompoms, ran into the field, and let out a whoop. "Let me hear you people! Goooooo Stonehill!" she sang out at the top of her lungs.

"We all know Stonehill needs a team mascot, and this is your special halftime surprise. We brought a friend from Ravenswood, and with a little papier-mâché magic, she's going to bring Stonehill to victory. Yay!"

The stands erupted in wild cheers. "Stonehill, Stonehill!"

Mrs. Windor was forced to a stop as curious kids pushed forward, blocking her way.

"What's everyone think of the Stonehill Unicorn?" Kara yelled out.

"Awesome!"

"That thing really showed the Evanston Eagle what's what!"

"Stonehill rules!"

Emily smiled. Yes! Kara was a genius. Nobody would realize that they'd just seen a real-life unicorn.

Unless, of course, Emily couldn't get Lorelei out of there in time.

Emily slowly walked to within two feet of the unicorn. "Easy. It's only me," she said as calmly as possible. Lorelei's frightened eyes darted back and forth between Emily and the surrounding football players. Then Emily realized she was still holding her flute. She stared at it. Could it work?

She had to try. Raising the instrument to her lips, she took a deep breath and blew the first few notes of their song.

The flute's music was soft and lilting, easily swallowed up by the hoots and hollers of the crowd. Still, Emily closed her eyes and played on, focusing on the music. As the gentle notes drifted out of the flute, Emily imagined them moving to Lorelei in slow, serene, rhythmic waves. Even with her eyes closed, she could sense that her jewel was pulsing steadily in time with the music.

Someone nearby shouted something about calling Animal Control. She thought she heard Rea yelling that *she* was supposed to solo and, for a second, Emily's concentration wavered.

She forced down panic. Focusing her energy again, she tried to form her thoughts into a song, a lyric to go with the music she was playing.

Hear my words
Feel the magic in them
In friendship we are bound
I'll always be around
You and me
It's meant to be
We'll always be
Friends Forever

Emily opened her eyes. Lorelei's head was lifted again, the breeze playing with her silky forelock. The unicorn's eyes locked on Emily's. Still playing, Emily took a step toward the exit. The unicorn stood still for a moment, then finally took a hesitant step, following Emily. Surprised murmurs from the crowd surrounded her as Emily, like a modern Pied Piper, led the creature through the exit and out to the grassy area beyond the playing field. Behind her, she heard the crowd break into cheers as the game resumed.

Emily faced Lorelei. She raised her hand and gently stroked the creature's velvety cheek.

"You came to me," she said wonderingly, tears welling up in her eyes.

Lorelei nodded. *"Emily hurt."*

"No. I'm okay. You have to get out of here, now. Please."

Lorelei looked deep into Emily's eyes. *"Friends forever."*

With a last wild snort, the unicorn turned and raced away.

Emily stood and watched her friend vanish.

12

"*H*OW COULD A horn suddenly appear when it wasn't there yesterday?" Adriane asked as the girls made their way to the secret glade behind Ravenswood Manor.

"I don't know," Emily replied. "Unicorns have strong magic, right? So maybe they can do that. Just grow another horn, I mean."

Kara shrugged. "Okay, but what happened to her original horn? And why in the world would she decide to show up at the game like that? I doubt that unicorns—if that's really what she is—are big football fans." She snorted. "We're just lucky everyone bought that lame mascot story."

"That was quick thinking, Barbie," Adriane admitted, giving Kara a sidelong glance.

"Thanks, Xena." Kara looked pleased.

"She came because she thought I needed help," Emily told them.

"I thought you were helping *her*," Kara said.

"There's something I haven't told you guys yet," Emily said, slowing her steps.

Adriane and Kara stopped and faced Emily.

"Spill it, girl," Kara said sternly, crossing her arms.

"She came because, I—I guess she thought I was in trouble." Emily shrugged uncertainly.

"And why would you be in trouble?" Kara asked.

Emily gulped. "I—I think there may be something following me. Something bad."

"What are you talking about?" Adriane demanded.

Emily regretted not telling them sooner. Just ahead, the immense Rocking Stone rose up through the trees, its spindly peak pointing the way to the portal field. As they walked toward it, she quickly filled them in on the mysterious, ghoulish figure that had appeared at the football game, and the strange musical sounds she'd been hearing.

"You should have said something to us earlier," Adriane said angrily.

"I'm really sorry," Emily replied. "I didn't know if it was real or not."

"Especially after what Zach told us!" Adriane continued.

"Yes, yes, I know."

"Are you sure it was right there in the bleachers?" Kara asked. "I didn't notice anything."

"And just how many times have you seen this thing?" Adriane asked.

"Three." Emily looked sheepishly at her friend's startled faces.

Adriane and Kara exchanged glances.

"That's real enough," Kara said.

"Tell us more about the music," Adriane suggested.

Emily tried to explain what had happened, the magical explosion in her room, the waves hitting her in the field, the garbled noise turning to clear, crisp sounds from Lorelei. And the strange music that had hypnotized her, had made her feel so peaceful, without a care in the world.

"Let's summarize, shall we?" Kara took over. "Lorelei was changing colors and made loud, awful noises. Then she shows up with a horn, looking all beautiful and making sweet music."

"Right."

"Then the monster thingy starts making different music, like a spell," Kara continued.

"Yes, it was like being under a spell," Emily agreed.

"And then Lorelei shows up at the game and saves you from this monster's spell," Adriane jumped in.

"I think that's what happened."

"So why is the monster after you?" Kara asked.

"I don't know. Maybe it's after Lorelei, not me."

"Let's say Lorelei *is* a unicorn." Adriane sighed. "How did she get here?"

"What do you mean?" Emily blinked. "She came through the portal with the other animals."

"First of all, unicorns don't need portals." Kara counted on her fingers. "Second of all, how come it's not coming to me?"

Adriane and Emily regarded her.

"What! I *am* the one with unicorn experience, you know."

"Jealous, Rapunzel?" Adriane teased. "Emily has a deep empathy with animals—she's obviously feeling the pain of this creature," she continued seriously.

Emily tried to explain. "It's like we feel each other's pain."

"How did she get past the Dark Sorceress?" Kara asked. "We know she's trying to get her hands on magical animals—trying to steal all their magic. She was after *my* unicorn, right? So why would she just let one leave Aldenmor?"

"Maybe Lorlelei escaped," Adriane suggested.

"Hiding with the others, she snuck through." Emily continued the train of thought. "And this monster is now after her."

"Makes sense," Adriane said.

"So what happened to her horn?" Kara asked.

"I don't know—it's part of the mystery."

Kara tugged at a lock of blond hair. "We need to find out what it is, and if it's dangerous," she said. "As president of the Ravenswood Preservation Society, I hereby call an executive meeting. We need some magical opinions."

"Agreed," Adriane said. "Let's gather the troops."

The girls walked through the natural arch of trees to the Rocking Stone and on past into the magic glade.

"I didn't know you played the flute," Kara mentioned to Emily.

"Yeah."

"Adriane plays guitar—maybe we should form a band."

"And what would *you* do?" Adriane asked.

"Lead singer, of course. La *laaa!*" Kara crooned.

Adriane covered her ears. "Well, we'd be a smash at the Pet Palace."

The three girls laughed. Kara and Adriane entwined their arms with Emily's and walked into the wondrous glade together. Emily felt better, at least for the moment. With her friends at her side, nothing could harm her.

"THIS MEETING OF the Ravenswood Wildlife Preservation Society is now in session!" Kara declared, walking back and forth as she surveyed the large crowd of animals and creatures. Emily, Adriane, Storm, and Lyra sat on the bank of the small rippling stream that emptied into the still, glassy pond. A dozen quiffles perched on the delicate bridge that arched gracefully over the stream. Other creatures—jeeran, pegasi, brimbees, wommels, and more—were sitting or standing on the leaf-strewn grass surrounding the water.

"Everyone's met the newcomers, and I'm glad you've all settled in," Kara continued.

"Beautiful princess!" a breathless voice sang out, interrupting her. Ghyll sprang out from behind a fir tree, followed by Ozzie. The flobbin hopped speedily over to Kara. "I'm here. I came as soon as I heard your call. Won't you please allow me to apologize for my tardiness with a nice big kiss?"

Kara brushed him away with a wave of her arms. "Not now, I'm busy."

"When would be a good time, O goddess of magic?"

"How about never? Does never work for you?"

Lyra stepped in front of Kara, leaving no doubt as to the time frame involved. The others all gestured for Ghyll to sit down and keep quiet.

Ozzie sat next to Emily. "You know," he muttered as Ghyll took a place by the pond, "I'm starting to think there's something a little odd about that guy."

"Quiet, please." Kara paced back and forth, hands behind her back. "How can I concentrate? We've got an evil creature that's here right now, you know!"

The crowd gasped. Murmurs of dismay rippled through the gathered creatures.

"Don't panic," Emily called out. "We just need to figure out what it could be."

"Right." Kara hopped up on a large, flat rock at the edge of the pond.

"What kind of monster are we talking about?" Balthazar asked.

Emily stood up and gave a quick description of the thing she'd seen.

"Could it be a banshee?" a brimbee asked.

"No, we know what those look like." Emily shuddered at the memory of the ragged, green-skinned, red-eyed hags that had attacked them not long ago. "This creature had pale white skin and black eyes and was sort of bony."

"A night stalker!" another voice cried.

Ronif shook his head. "No, no," he said. "They have yellow eyes, and their skin is black as midnight."

"That creature who ran away, the one who made the horrible noise," a wommel called out. "We haven't seen it since we got here. *That's* your monster!"

"We think that creature may be a unicorn," Emily said.

"A unicorn. Here?"

Gasps of wonder broke out among the crowd.

"Surely with the magic of a unicorn, we need not worry about a monster," a brimbee said.

"They can travel freely on the web itself," another

quiffle explained. "They don't need a portal or anything. Why would it be here?"

"We're not sure she *is* a unicorn, yet," Kara said.

"This monster made beautiful music. I can't explain it—it was hypnotic," Emily continued. "I forgot about everything else when I heard it."

"It has to be a harpy," Balthazar said.

"Or a siren, creatures that use beautiful music to lure victims," Rasha added.

"There's a famous painting, The Sirens of Waterknell, hanging on the wall at my cousin Brommy's place," Ozzie said excitedly. "I'm sure you must have noticed it, Ghyll?"

"Of course," Ghyll replied immediately. "It's quite striking."

Emily noticed a weird look cross Ozzie's face.

"Sirens always take the form of beautiful maidens; they're not ghoulish," Balthazar pointed out. "But they do use similar magic as harpies."

"Oh, no, a harpy is here?" someone cried in a frightened voice.

"A harpy spirited my brother away."

"Calm down!" Kara's voice broke through the commotion. "What's a hippy?"

Once again there was an eruption of responses.

"Harpy."

" . . . hideous beastie . . ."

" . . . song that can lure anyone to their doom . . ."

" . . . horrible, gaping eyes of death . . ."

"Harpies are birdlike creatures that weave spells using musical enchantments," Balthazar explained. "They lull victims into a state of mindlessness and then take control of them—make them do their bidding."

"They use music as magic?" Emily asked.

"Music can be a potent form of magical energy," Balthazar continued. "The right sounds or combinations of sounds can have a strong influence on magic and those who use magic."

All around the glade, heads were nodding.

Ghyll stepped forward. "The harpy's music creates a beautiful vision, sort of a dreamtime state—disguising it just long enough to get close so it can attack. Only those with powerful magic of their own can see the harpy's true form." He nodded toward Emily.

A lot of things were starting to make sense now. Emily remembered the weird, dreamlike spell the music had thrown over her, the exquisite illusion she'd spotted briefly in the forest. "What are we supposed to do?" she demanded, pushing the images away. "What if this thing is after Lorelei?"

"You're the only one who's seen it. Maybe it's after you," Ghyll suggested.

"When the Dark Sorceress tried to get the unicorn last time, she tried to use *me*. Maybe now she's trying to use *you*," Kara put in, nodding.

"Catch it and send it back through the portal!" an agitated voice cried from the crowd.

"Yes! It's the only way!" someone else called.

"We can't send Lorelei back to Aldenmor and into the Dark Sorceress's hands," Adriane said sharply.

"Maybe we can," Ghyll said.

"Why do you say that?"

"Unicorns are at the top of the magic chain," the flobbin explained. "As the beautiful princess pointed out"—he gave Kara a little bow—"the Dark Sorceress couldn't get a unicorn on her own. If the creature *is* a unicorn, it should be able to handle the sorceress just fine. If it's *not*, she won't pay any attention to it anyway. So everybody wins."

Kara blinked. "Unless, of course—" She stopped.

"Unless what?"

Kara paced back and forth again. "Unless the Dark Sorceress knows the unicorn thing is here." She raised a finger in the air. "What if she *sent* it?"

An anxious murmur swept through the crowd.

"No!" Emily cried. "The thing I saw—it's definitely evil!"

"Ribbit." Ghyll cleared his throat. "There is another possibility. If this harpy is particularly powerful, it might be able to shape shift."

"Harpies can change their shape?" Adriane asked.

"Some," Ghyll said. "If their magic is strong."

"Then maybe Lorelei *is* the harpy," Adriane concluded unhappily.

"No, no, no!" Emily shook her head.

"The Dark Sorceress would send only the most powerful of her magic trackers to this world," Ghyll warned. "It is possible that a powerful harpy could make itself look like a unicorn."

"So you're saying this so-called unicorn could be something else in disguise," Kara said. "Something evil."

"It's not just possible—it's likely," Ghyll replied. "You have seen a real unicorn?"

"Yes," Kara answered.

"Then you know this is not unicorn behavior. What kind of unicorn would cause this kind of trouble?"

"Good question," Adriane murmured, shooting Emily a sidelong glance.

"No," Emily protested, overwhelmed by all the new information.

"Then why did she just disappear?" a quiffle asked.

"Why is she hiding?" a brimbee added.

"I don't know," Emily replied, exasperated. "Maybe Lorelei is different." She was surprised and a little annoyed at the way her friends were acting. "It's not like we've met hundreds of unicorns. How do we know they all act alike? People don't. Just look at you two, for example." She gestured at Adriane and Kara.

Kara shook her head impatiently. "Whatever. The point is, unicorn or not, your new friend has been acting—well, odd."

"So what?" Emily argued. "The *point* is, I don't care

what she is. I know she's in trouble, and I know I have to help!"

"We're the ones in trouble," Adriane said bluntly. "If any more magical creatures go bursting out in public, the Ravenswood Preserve is history!"

Emily frowned and picked at the lush grass growing beside the stream. Adriane was right. If they couldn't control the animals at the preserve, how were they supposed to keep it from being shut down, and Adriane from losing her home?

"It wasn't Lorelei's fault," she blurted. "She was just confused. She was trying to find me. Anyway, nobody got hurt."

"Just barely," Adriane said, her brow set in a stubborn line. "It's not like we don't have enough problems to deal with right now as it is."

She didn't go into detail, but Emily knew exactly what her friend was thinking about, because they were all thinking about it. They were running out of time to replace the dreamcatcher. Horrible images flashed unbidden through her mind—the gaping jaw of the monstrous manticore, the vicious glare of the Dark Sorceress—and she shuddered.

"We can't control how the portal opens and closes," Adriane said, standing up and facing the crowd. "But when the dreamcatcher was there, at least it kept anything evil out. As long as the portal remains unprotected, we're all in danger from something else slipping through."

"If anyone sees anything unusual, it should be reported to Storm or Lyra right away," Kara said.

"But until we get some answers, we give Lorelei the benefit of the doubt," Adriane announced, giving Emily a smile. "One thing I do know," she continued, putting her hand in Emily's. "Whatever happens, we stand together with Emily."

Everyone voiced agreement.

"That okay with you, Sherlock?" Adriane asked Kara.

"Absolutely, Watson," Kara replied, folding her hand over Adriane's and Emily's.

Emily smiled gratefully, feeling the magic of friendship flow through her. Deep inside her, she also felt the bond tighten between herself and Lorelei. She knew something had happened to Lorelei, something terrible and traumatic. If only the unicorn would trust her enough to tell her about it.

Until then, they could only wait for the monster to make its next move.

13

*S*UN STREAMED THROUGH the large windows of the library in Ravenswood Manor, illuminating the rich mahogany shelves and the rows upon rows of leather-bound books. Emily paced back and forth, thinking. Adriane sat at the computer console, checking over the list of new arrivals and running through pages of emails that had backed up over the past few days. Even if the tours weren't making much of an impact, the website had been a big hit, attracting friends from all over the world.

"Em, Meilin sends you her regards," Adriane called out. "Here's one from Max in Acapulco. He thinks his dog is talking again."

"That's silly—animals don't talk," Ozzie commented lazily. He was sunning himself on the window ledge.

The door opened and Kara bounded in. "Hey, kids, I got good news and bad news. The good news is everyone congratulated me on the cool mascot at yesterday's game, even if it was just a horse with a party hat on its head." She winked.

Emily winced. She was beginning to wish it *was* just a party hat, and not a real unicorn horn.

"And the bad news?" Adriane asked.

"The bad new is Mrs. Windor—she's on a rampage. She wants an inspection."

"What?" Adriane was outraged. "That's all we need— Mrs. Windor snooping around out here!"

"What we need is the council's permission to set up the Ravenswood benefit concert." Kara reminded her. "The only way we get it is if she thinks we have everything under control."

Adriane sprang to her feet. "We've got harpies, wommels, and flobbins!"

Ozzie perked up. "Harpies, wommels, and flobbins? Oh my!"

"The benefit concert will put Ravenswood on the map!" Kara pointed out. "Besides, she's coming whether we like it or not."

"Well, everyone is accounted for," Adriane said. Then she looked at Emily, adding, "Except for Lorelei," she added.

"Emily, you've *got* to find her," Kara said.

"I know," Emily said.

EMILY PAUSED AT the tree line and glanced back. With a sigh, she turned away and continued on into the woods. She needed time to think, to process everything she'd learned.

At least they knew what they were dealing with: a harpy. That was what she'd seen. But was it following her, or was it after Lorelei?

Despite their support, her friends were not sure Lorelei was what she seemed to be. And who could blame them? Since coming through the portal, Lorelei had demonstrated complete lack of control over her magic. The unicorn had uprooted trees and flung rocks around, busted into a football game, and beheaded a mascot—not to mention leading Emily herself on more than one wild-goose chase. Still, nothing could erase the memory of the connection she had felt with the beautiful wild creature. Emily felt Lorelei's pain as the unicorn felt hers. There was no way she could be anything but good!

Emily sank down onto a rock just off the trail, her head swirling with so many questions she couldn't think straight. She buried her face in her hands. This was too much for her. She'd have been better off staying in

Colorado, better off if she'd never heard of the magic web or quiffles or unicorns or any of the rest of it. If only this wasn't so hard . . .

Cheenngg.

A quiet chord, like a question, sang out from somewhere nearby. Emily lifted her head. "Hello?" she whispered uncertainly.

Cheenngggg.

Emily stood up. Her jewel was glowing. As she watched, the rainbow colors grew brighter and brighter until they flowed together into a pale, almost clear white light.

When the chord came again, Emily turned toward it. For a second she hesitated, thinking of how deceptive the sounds of the harpy could be.

For some reason, her father's voice floated into her head—*Don't be afraid to really feel it.*

She *had* dared to feel, to connect with Lorelei, and now she had to follow through on that connection. Lorelei was calling to her, needed her. That was enough to convince her that the risk was worth it.

She stepped forward, following the music. It led her off the trail and through the woods. After a few minutes, she saw a brighter patch of sunlight ahead. She pushed through and emerged into a lush meadow. Wild flowers filled the air in swirls of color.

Lorelei was standing there, waiting for her. She looked magnificent. Her coat was white as snow; her long silky mane was blowing in the breeze; and atop her forehead, her magnificent horn sparkled like diamonds in the sunlight.

Lorelei stared at her. Emily stared back, holding her breath, afraid that the unicorn would run away. Slowly she sat down in the tall grass, crossing her legs in front of her. It was up to Lorelei now. Emily had answered her call, but she wasn't going to chase her anymore.

For a long, breathless moment, the two looked into each other's eyes.

Then Lorelei stepped forward. She walked up to Emily and gazed down at her. She exhaled in a long sigh, and inside her head, Emily heard a breath of tinkling bells, with a barely audible word wrapped inside the notes. *"Emily."*

"I'm here," Emily whispered.

Lorelei knelt down in the grass, then sank to the ground. With another long sigh, she lowered her head, resting it in Emily's lap.

Emily stared, transfixed by the beauty of the unicorn. The wondrous crystalline horn sparkled just inches from her face. Hardly daring to breathe, she raised her hand and stroked the unicorn's silky head. Lorelei trembled but stayed where she was. Tiny bursts of magical energy danced around the horn.

"What happened, Lorelei?" Emily asked.

Lorelei shuddered again. A burst of melody swirled from the horn, as bright, white-hot emotions seared an

image in Emily's mind: pathways of stars, exquisite patterns spiraling endlessly into the distance.

Emily squeezed her eyes shut, her head pounding from the intensity of the feelings. "Tell me. It's all right."

Lorelei raised her head and gazed at Emily, her eyes filled with despair. This time the words floated into Emily's mind in somber harmony, like a dirge, a swirling mass of notes in a minor key, so sad her eyes immediately filled with tears.

"The web is dying."

In her mind, Emily saw circular pathways crumbling. Between smoking, gaping holes was the blackness of nothing. All at once it became clear. The map of stars was an image of the magic web itself, the system of pathways connecting worlds, allowing magic to flow from one place to another.

This time the music was little more than a breath of melody.

"I am ashamed."

Emily shook her head, more confused than ever. "I don't understand."

She waited. A second later, the images started to come.

Lorelei, dancing joyously along highways of gleaming threads. Music and magic radiating from her—from her beautiful horn. As she danced, magic from her horn wove new patterns, creating new pathways, and joy filled her.

"You make the web?" Emily asked.

"Unicorns heal the web and keep it strong. Our magic weaves the strands."

"You heal the web. I can almost see the magic fitting together in patterns, like when I use my healing magic. It's so beautiful."

The next image shook Emily as she watched a spiral of web collapse upon itself, strands disintegrating.

The beautiful web Lorelei had spun became weaker and weaker, damaged parts unraveling like a badly frayed rope, falling away, vanishing.

Lorelei breathed out another sad, aching chord. *"It is my fault. Soon the destruction will spread all across the web. I have failed."*

"How could this happen?" Emily blurted, still confused.

Lorelei trembled. *"I lost my magic."*

The unicorn hung her head in shame.

Emily hesitated, afraid that her next question would send the unicorn running off again. But she needed to know. "What happened to your horn?" she whispered.

She felt the unicorn's body tense. But Lorelei stayed where she was. Her limpid eyes closed, and she breathed out a long, weary, out-of-tune sigh.

A dark, sickly-green wave spreading, blotting out the stars . . . darkness engulfing Lorelei, covering the unicorn, trapping her in a net of green fire.

A tall figure in dark robes, long silver hair slashed by lightning.

Emily's eyes flew open. "The Dark Sorceress!" she cried.

More images burst into Emily's mind, so fast she could hardly follow them.

An exhausted Lorelei, brought before the sorceress in a dark place. Two monstrous ogres standing on either side of the unicorn.

The sorceress giving a sharp nod. The beasts lifting a huge, savage-looking ax. The vicious blade caught a fiery reflection as it hung in the air, poised over the unicorn like a guillotine.

Emily squeezed her hands against her ears as an unearthly shriek filled her head. A scream of sheer anguish and humiliation as the blade slashed downward.

"No!" she cried. The unicorn's scream exploded inside of Emily's head, a deafening chorus of agony. Emily cried out along with Lorelei, slumping to the brittle grass.

But the images kept coming.

Laughing triumphantly, the Dark Sorceress held up her prize—the gleaming, crystalline horn of the unicorn.

Lorelei, hornless now, running in wild-eyed terror as fearsome Black Fire coursed uncontrolled through her magic. Her beautiful white coat shifted through colors to try and shield her from the poison. Blazing red, orange, then purple, she staggering hopelessly over the ravaged web, not seeing or caring where she was going, tumbling at last through a portal.

"Oh, no!" Emily gasped in horror.

She stared at the unicorn, tears streaming down her face. Lorelei was gazing at her sadly.

Emily gently reached out and touched Lorelei's horn.

"You are a healer. You helped me. I didn't know it would grow back."

"But it wasn't your fault," Emily said gently.

"I must fix what is broken."

"You mean the web?"

"That is what unicorns do."

"But is that creature still after you?"

"It hunts me still, but I must repair the damage or all will be in danger."

Lorelei got to her feet. She stood back and raised her head high. Magic spun from her horn, sparkling in the air, shimmering and glittering.

A sudden wind whipped Emily's curly hair around her head. Sparks of sound flared, bursting into bright lights. She shielded her eyes as the light grew brighter and brighter, filling the meadow, and finally exploding into bolts of lightning.

The air itself seemed to tear apart as a huge, dark opening yawned where a moment ago there had been nothing but fallen leaves and empty air.

Emily braced herself against the wind.

She got to her feet, transfixed by the tunnel of swirling stars—the magic web.

"I must go back." Lorelei's voice was frantic, terrified.

"No!" Emily shouted above the wild, zinging sound of the spinning vortex. "It's too dangerous!"

The unicorn shuddered, sending out music that filled Emily's head with fragmented chords and words that were little more than broken cries. *We share magic now. You can always find me.*

"Yes," Emily said. Her heart constricted with fear.

Something tickled at her mind. A snaking sound penetrating into her very being. Music, so calm, so soothing . . .

Lorelei snorted and took a step back.

Emily turned and faced the monster.

The harpy stood across the field, its ghoulish face white as death. Blazing eyes glowed like dying embers.

Run, Lorelei, Emily wanted to cry out, but she couldn't. She couldn't move.

"Thank you for bringing me the unicorn," the thing said, smiling through broken yellow teeth.

Lorelei looked at Emily, her liquid eyes stricken and confused.

"No," Emily cried to Lorelei. "I didn't know! I didn't know it was following me."

"I will take the beast now," the harpy interrupted in its silky, slithering voice. "We have work to finish." The creature's arm emerged from under its cloak, revealing a glittering horn. It shone with a dull green glow.

Lorelei stepped back in horror at the sight of her own horn poisoned with Black Fire.

"Emily!"

Emily turned toward the shout and saw Kara and Adriane running toward her. Ozzie, Storm, Ghyll, and Lyra were right behind them.

"You were right, Storm. The portal's opened!" Ozzie cried.

"Stay away from her!" Adriane yelled. "Kara, we have to—"

Wreeeeeeaaaaaaaaaarrrrrnnnnn!

A burst of chilling, bone-rattling music exploded over the meadow, drowning out the rest of Adriane's words. Emily turned and saw the harpy waving the green unicorn horn.

Lorelei reared, terrified.

"You've got to stop it!" Emily shouted to her friends. "The monster is taking Lorelei!"

Stormbringer was the first to react. With a savage growl, the mistwolf leaped after the monstrous harpy, teeth bared.

The harpy turned, its mesmerizing eyes focusing on Storm. Its vicious song changed suddenly, becoming softer, eerily mesmerizing. Storm skidded to a stop right in front of the creature. She stared at it for a long moment. Then her tongue lolled out of her mouth, and she sank down onto her haunches. Her golden eyes glazed over, and she stared at the harpy adoringly.

Emily realized what was happening. "Wake up!" she screamed at Storm as the harpy glided closer, still singing. "Don't listen to the music!" When the mistwolf didn't respond, she turned toward her friends. "You've got to help her!"

To her horror, she saw that her friends were standing in place, staring trance-like toward the harpy. Kara's mouth was hanging open slightly, and Adriane was swaying unsteadily to the rhythm of the creature's song. Ozzie and Ghyll were leaning on each other, their eyes half closed, while Lyra purred loudly and rolled onto her back.

Oh, no! Emily felt her own heartbeat slowing, matching itself to the beat of the harpy's captivating song. Her friends were already bewitched, and now she was falling under its evil spell, too.

Maybe I should . . . just . . . give up, Emily thought fuzzily. Easier . . . just to . . . go along with it . . .

"Lorelei," she cried, summoning one last ounce of resolve. Her voice, too, seemed overtaken by the harpy's powerful magic, and she sang out, "Lor-e-lei!"

The monster's music changed rhythm, becoming quicker, almost violent, yet still beautiful.

Music exploded in a painful jumble of noise as the unicorn struggled to express herself. *"Emily, focus on my voice. Stay awake."*

Lorelei's voice broke through the fuzziness, and Emily managed to shake off most of the effects of the spell. However, the others were still entranced. The harpy hovered in the air between Emily and the portal, grinning as it continued to sing.

Magic crackled and popped, forming a ring of shimmering blackish-green energy around the unicorn, trapping her.

"Run, Lorelei!"

The unicorn snorted and tried to bolt, her eyes rolling back with fear.

Emily watched as the harpy swept toward Lorelei, skimming just above the grass. Its shadowy dark cloak billowed around its gaunt shoulders, and its yellow teeth formed a hideous grin as its eyes bored into Emily. The unicorn backed away and reared up, her silvery hooves flashing. But the harpy didn't slow. It reached out its arms and wrapped Lorelei in its evil embrace, sweeping her into the portal.

14

"*W*AKE UP!" EMILY screamed, running toward her friends. "You've got to fight it!"

She shook Kara by the shoulders. The blond girl stared listlessly, as if looking right through Emily.

Behind them the animals of Ravenswood came running into the field.

"Everyone!" Emily called out. "I need your help!" She pointed to Adriane, Kara, Ozzie, Storm, Lyra, and Ghyll. "Form a circle around them."

Emily raised her jewel and concentrated on drawing in the magic of the animals around her. The rainbow jewel flared blue, and Emily held it before Kara, bathing her in bright light.

Kara's eyes cleared, and she looked at Emily. "What happened?" She blinked.

"The harpy put us under its spell," Emily explained.

With Kara's help, Emily quickly used the power of her jewel and their animal friends to break the spell. One by one, each shook off lingering wisps of hypnotic music.

"Where's Lorelei?" Adriane asked, looking at the spinning portal still hanging open in the air before them.

"The harpy took her," Emily told her, frantically. "We have to go after her!"

Adriane shook her head. "Are you crazy?"

"It's starting to close," Ozzie called out.

The portal was spinning in on itself, shrinking.

"Emily," Adriane said, "we can't just jump through! What if we end up in the Shadowlands of Aldenmor— or worse?"

Emily tried to explain how important this was. "The whole magic web is at stake," she told them, her voice thick with tension and fear. "Lorelei is supposed to protect the web. If she can't repair it quickly, it's going to keep falling apart!"

"But going into the portal—it's too dangerous," Ozzie said.

"I'm going through!" Emily said defiantly.

"How will we find Lorelei even if we do go through?" Kara asked.

"I can find her," Emily stated. "I have to."

Ghyll stepped forward. "I am a fairy creature, a magic

tracker. If we go right now, I can help find the unicorn on the web."

"I don't know," Ozzie said. "It sounds risky."

"I went through once before," Adriane reminded the others. "My wolf stone protected me."

"What will happen to the web, to Aldenmor and the Fairimentals, if we don't help Lorelei?" Emily asked. "We have to decide now!"

She glanced at the portal. In a few moments it would be gone.

"One jumps, we all jump!" Adriane announced.

"Why I listen to you two is beyond me," Kara said.

"Storm, you and Lyra stay here and take care of the others," Adriane ordered.

"I will contact you if I do not hear from you," Storm told her.

"Hold onto me," Gyhll said.

The three girls grabbed hold of Ghyll as he took a mighty hop.

"Wait for me!" Ozzie yelled.

Emily reached out. Ozzie leaped and grabbed hold as they jumped through the misty veil and fell into the portal.

The flobbin drifted in space. Kara, Emily, Adriane, and Ozzie floated alongside. They seemed to be encased in a gold-and-blue bubble. The amber glow of the wolf stone and the blue-green glow of the rainbow jewel filled the bubble. Outside, streaks of light swept by as the bubble flew across an endless ribbon of stars.

Ghyll was concentrating on the rows of blazing lights that flew towards them. "To the left," he called.

Adriane and Emily shifted their stones to the left, and the bubble turned, careening into a connecting path of starlight.

Emily's eyes were wide with astonishment. Long, wide swaths of glowing light, like highways, spiraled and stretched, searing past them at enormous speed.

"Right!" Ghyll ordered.

The girls shifted their stones, banking the bubble right, where it soared onto another streaming path, flying out over the vast web.

"This is amazing," Emily exclaimed.

"I remember actually riding on the strands of the web," Kara said, referring to her wild unicorn ride. "But this is intense!"

"Are we there yet?" Ozzie covered his eyes as the bubble dipped, then dropped down a vertical well of looping

strands, spinning upside down and jumping forward once again. *"GarG!"* The ferret was jolted into the air. "Doesn't this thing come with seatbelts?"

"Hurry, Ghyll," Emily cried.

"I can only track the unicorn," said the flobbin. "You can increase the speed with your magic."

"Hold on!" Kara touched her fingers to each of the jewels, and the bubble shot forward like a rocket.

"Ahhhh!" Ozzie cried out.

The bubble sped across the web like a shooting star, arcing towards an intersection of pathways. A wide platform of light floated where the highways met.

"There!" Ghyll called out.

"Where? Which one?" Adriane asked.

"All of them." He pointed.

Emily and Adriane moved their jewels, and the bubble slid into an approaching pathway. Bouncing slightly, they came to a halt on the edge of the platform. The bubble flared and disappeared.

Splashes of light danced behind Emily's eyes, inside her head. Music filled the air—bright, brilliant, enormous, as if the universe itself were singing.

Emily opened her eyes, awestruck. They stood on an immense, circular platform, looking out upon the web itself. The magic web! An endless array of gleaming strands stretched out in every direction, woven into impossibly complex patterns. At every intersection, tiny glittering stars twinkled with pure white energy. When she looked down, Emily realized the platform was made of thousands of tightly woven strands. The platform formed the base of a giant circle, surrounded by connecting strands of the web. Smoke plumed from various places along the pathways. Upon closer inspection, she could see that sections of the web had been burned away. Loose strands unraveled as sparking embers of green glow spread from the edges—Black Fire. Through the gaping holes she could see where sections of starways crumbled and burned, falling away into the black of nothingness. Even the flobbin seemed stunned by the devastation of the ruined web.

"Where are we?" Adriane asked.

"A nexus," Ghyll said quietly.

"A what?"

"There are sections of the web where many paths converge in one place," Ghyll explained. "This is a nexus."

"Like a train station," Emily said.

"If you follow the right path, you can jump to different places, worlds."

"Is it safe here?" Kara asked.

"I've never seen the web destroyed before. It's terrible. And dangerously unstable." Ghyll shifted his flippers nervously.

"Where is Lorelei?" Emily asked, looking through the smoke that swirled from the base of the wide circle.

Ghyll pointed to the opposite edge. Clouds of smoke parted to reveal the unicorn standing beside the harpy.

Ribbons of glowing light streamed from Lorelei's crystal horn. Like a magnet, the pale green horn in the harpy's hand pulled the flowing magic toward it, warping the ribbons and sending them streaming outwards. A dreadful, whining music blared from the green horn. As the magic hit the pathways, the connecting silvery strands withered, sending up plumes of ugly, greenish smoke. Sections of web shifted, raveled, and unraveled, reconfiguring into a different pattern. The harpy laughed, buzzing with its evil song.

"What are they doing?" Kara asked.

"It looks like the harpy is using Lorelei's magic to reweave the web, to make a new pathway," Ghyll said.

Lorelei stood entranced, magic and music flowing from her horn in rich, deep, sad notes.

"Lorelei!" Emily called sharply.

The harpy swung to face them. The horn in its hand blazed a sickly green. "You are too late. The unicorn is under my spell. I will soon have the right pathway open."

The harpy began crooning soft music, beautiful and beguiling.

"You know what the sorceress wants, don't you, Ghyll?" it said to the flobbin.

"What are you talking about?" Adriane asked, feeling the enchantment of the harpy closing in.

"That fairy creature is not what it seems," the harpy hissed. "Who do you think turned him into a flobbin?"

"No!" Ghyll hopped forward. "You don't have to tell them!"

"Why not?" the harpy crooned. "It is time for secrets to be revealed. Ghyll is after the unicorn for himself, aren't you?"

Ghyll remained silent, looking at the others.

"I knew it!" yelled Ozzie, stomping over and kicking the flobbin. "Cousin Brommy doesn't have the Sirens of Waterknell. It's in the Hall of Elders! Everyone knows that!"

"So you tricked us," Emily said to the flobbin.

"I can explain—" Ghyll started.

"You wanted to send the unicorn to the Dark Sorceress!" Adriane yelled.

"It's not like—" Ghyll tried again.

"Of course it is," the harpy sang.

Emily felt the hypnotic magic reaching for them, trying to trap them under its spell. "Start yelling, singing—anything to break the spell!" she cried out.

Taking a deep breath, Emily opened her mouth and began to sing. At first, her voice was shaky and uncertain. As her confidence grew, the rainbow jewel flared with brilliant blue light. Colorful starbursts appeared all around her as Emily felt her own magic strengthening Lorelei's.

The horn in the harpy's hand sparked wildly as the connection with the unicorn faltered. The harpy narrowed its eyes and raised its voice.

Hopelessness gripped Emily in an icy grasp. Was she strong enough to save Lorelei?

Then Ozzie's reedy voice piped up, thin but clear. A moment later, Ghyll started croaking along in a deep bass.

Adriane stepped forward and raised her wolf stone. She tilted her head back and howled, the wolf song ringing out strong and sure. The harpy's magic wavered, the green horn dimmed. Kara looked at her friends, then stepped forward and opened her mouth, letting out a screech that made everyone cover their ears.

The harpy faltered, almost dropping the horn in fright. It cringed as Kara's voice hit it with a sudden, strong, magic force.

"Keep singing, Kara!" Emily yelled over her shoulder as she ran to Lorelei.

"La, *laaaa!*" Kara sang out.

"Go, girl!" Adriane called.

"La, La, *LAAAoooWAAA!*"

The harpy turned away, trying to shield itself from the awful music bombarding it.

"Emily." Doleful, forlorn music filled Emily's head. She could feel that Lorelei was deeply traumatized by having her own horn turned on her. How could Emily hope to help the unicorn through this?

If the spirit does not desire healing, Gran's voice said in her head, *no true healing can take place. If you want to help, you have to be willing to give the kind of help that's needed.*

Emily hugged the unicorn close. "I know how you feel," she said. "I lost my family—the life I was so sure of.

My parents split up, and I thought that was the end of everything good and safe."

"Laa, *LAAAAAooOOiEE!!*" Kara was advancing on the harpy, forcing the monster to cower in pain.

Emily focused on the unicorn. She had to make her understand, make her realize she wasn't alone.

"But just when I was ready to give up, I found Ravenswood, met Adriane and Kara and Ozzie," she went on. "And I realized I had magic inside of me. Strong magic that couldn't be taken away no matter what happened."

"My horn is everything."

"No, that's just it!" Emily remembered the confusion she had felt in Lorelei before her horn had come back— and also the power, the beautiful, strong, harmonious power laying just beneath the chaos.

"Your horn may focus your magic, like our jewels." She held up her wrist and stared at the rainbow stone, which was glowing softly with pastel colors. "But the real magic is inside of you. Right here." Emily touched her hand to Lorelei's chest, covering the unicorn's beating heart.

The music in Lorelei's head was uncertain.

Emily held the rainbow jewel out toward the unicorn's chest. Lorelei hesitated, then stepped forward to meet her touch. As soon as the jewel on Emily's wrist made contact, there was an explosion of chords, strong, magical bursts of sound that filled her and surrounded her, echoing across the nexus.

"Aaaaaarrrrrhhhhhh!"

The harpy's cry rolled toward them in a powerful, deadly wave of sound and energy as it flung its song like a weapon. Emily braced herself just in time as the wave barreled over her, but out of the corner of her eye she saw a section of platform flare with green fire and dissolve. Kara wobbled and slipped, her left leg disappearing into the nothingness!

"Kara!" Emily screamed, watching in horror as Kara lost her grip and slipped farther.

Emily and Adriane lunged toward their friend. With a snort, the unicorn's eyes flew open, and she spun around and raced to help. But Ghyll got there first. Locking his blue flippers around a strand of web, he flicked out his long purple tongue, wrapped it around Kara's arm, and hauled her up.

"I'm okay," she said shakily once she was back atop the web. She glanced down quickly and gulped. "No problem."

Lorelei's hooves flashed with golden fire as she danced across the hole in the web. Everywhere she touched, the broken strands healed, weaving back together and vibrating with life.

The harpy howled in fury and fired another sickly bolt of magic from the green horn.

"Look out!" Adriane shouted to Ozzie. Warrior and ferret leaped away, barely clearing the smoking hole ripped open beneath their feet.

"*Stop!*" Lorelei's voice rang in all their heads.

The harpy turned to her, eyes burning with greed and hate.

"Do not hurt them."

"Then give me what I want, unicorn."

"I will do as you ask."

"No, Lorelei, you can't," Emily cried.

"Do not interfere," the harpy commanded. "The unicorn will finish what we have started. Her horn was removed once. Do you want it to happen again?"

Emily felt waves of fear radiating from the unicorn.

She watched as Lorelei walked across the tightly woven strands. The unicorn shook her head, waving her crystal horn. A lovely melody drifted through the nexus. Pathways shifted, coming apart, unraveling. Strands rewound themselves into a new design.

And a bluish-white whirlpool appeared—and opened.

"Yes, that's it!" the harpy cried gleefully.

"It looks like another portal," Ozzie said.

This portal was about half the size of the one at Ravenswood. Blue haze covered the opening as streams of smoke fell eerily upon the nexus floor.

The harpy turned in triumph, raising its green horn high. "It is done. The path has been revealed."

"Go. You have what you want," Lorelei said.

An evil grin spread across the harpy's face. "You first."

Lorelei stepped backwards. *"I cannot."*

"You didn't think I would trust you, did you? Just in case you didn't follow the fairy map exactly, you will come with me. Besides, I'm sure you want to see the home of all magic, don't you?"

The girls looked at each other.

"Where does this portal lead?" Emily called out.

The harpy's look of malice made the girls cringe. "Where? To where all dreams come true. Avalon."

Whirling around, it flew towards the unicorn, knocking them both into the portal in a flash of foul, greenish energy. In an instant they were gone.

Avalon?

"If the Sorceress finds a way to get the magic of Avalon, all is lost," Ozzie cried, jumping up and down. "Everything the Fairimentals have worked for will have been for nothing!"

Kara, Emily, and Adriane stood side by side, looking at the misty opening that would lead them to the most mysterious and magical of all places.

"We must save the unicorn," Ghyll said firmly.

"We've come this far," Adriane said.

"Just one more," Emily added.

"One jumps, we all jump!" Kara said.

"Piece of pie," Ozzie concluded.

Emily reached out and clasped hands with Adriane and Kara. "Let's do it!" she exclaimed.

The five of them surged toward the portal. As they reached it, Emily took a deep breath, squeezed her eyes shut, and jumped.

15

THUMP.
Thump.
Thump.
Thump.
Splooof!

Emily opened her eyes. Her friends scattered around her—in a glistening, gleaming dreamworld. Enormous snowflakes, soft and pillowy white, drifted lazily up, down, and all around them. When one landed on her arm, instead of cold, she felt a soft, soothing warmth, that spread through her with a glorious sense of well-being.

"I . . . know this place," she whispered.

Adriane shook her head, staring out at the silvery-blue

landscape. They were in a valley surrounded by rolling blue hills. Thick, billowy purple clouds floated above them, releasing the giant snowflakes. The valley floor was covered in soft, fine sand that sparkled like quartz. "It must be another world," she replied, her voice hushed with awe. "Like Earth, or Aldenmor."

"This can't be Avalon!" Kara said.

"I don't know," Emily whispered, looking for Lorelei. "I saw this place in a dream. I think I'm supposed to be here."

"Are you all right?" Ghyll asked Ozzie, who was scraping himself up from the sand.

"What's it to you?" Ozzie kicked the flobbin.

Ghyll looked flustered. "I'm sorry I lied to you."

"Yeah, sure. Save it for the Sorceress!" Ozzie brushed himself off.

Just then the sounds of music blared in the distance. Harsh, deep, piercing blasts, clashing like sounds of battle.

"Lorelei!" Emily exclaimed. "Come on!"

The five ran across the fine sand and rounded a bend in the silver hills. Suddenly a hideous scream ripped through the landscape. An overwhelming eruption of energy sent the snowflakes skidding away.

In front of them, Lorelei stood, facing the harpy. The monster was pointing the sickly green horn at the unicorn.

"You tricked me!" it screamed, enraged. "This is not Avalon!"

"No, it is not."

"Open the right portal. Now!" The harpy waved the

green horn frantically. Sparks of fire jumped from the horn, but before they could reach Lorelei, they seemed to lose focus, splintering away in the misty breeze.

"Lorelei!" Emily called out.

The harpy watched the girls approach. It hissed, its ghoulish, white face twisted with fury.

It aimed the green horn at them, trying to build a wave of magic. Emily felt the tingling sensations rush through her as the power intensified. She had felt this before, at the football field and in the woods. "Stand back," she warned the others.

Adriane swung her arm up, releasing a trail of golden fire from her jewel. She spun around, whipping the fire into a ring of blazing magic. Feet planted firmly, she threw the ring at the harpy. The magic arced through the air and slammed into the harpy with an explosion of golden light.

It staggered back, as if trying to deflect the warrior's magic with the green horn. Instead, the horn absorbed the golden fire. The harpy pulled the horn down, sending the magic back at the group.

"Look out!" Ozzie yelled.

Everyone dove to the ground as the wave crashed over them with an eerie, wailing sound.

The harpy strained to lock onto more magic from the girls' stones.

Adriane leaped to her feet, arms raised for another attack.

Ghyll bounced back up. "Wait! The horn will draw magic from your jewels. You mustn't use them."

"You seem to know an awful lot about unicorns, frog face!" Ozzie yelled.

"I have studied them for years," Ghyll told the ferret.

"Well, study *this!*" Ozzie kicked the flobbin again.

"If one way doesn't work, try another," Emily called out.

Suddenly Lorelei raised her head and released clear, clean sounds of music. The notes echoed over the barren terrain.

The harpy held the green horn high. "I will control your magic!"

Lorelei's music spilled across the valley. Achingly beautiful, the song wove notes of pure feeling, echoing the joy, sorrow, and loss inside the unicorn.

Emily recognized the song instantly. It was the song she had heard in her dream. Her song.

She started to sing, adding her voice to the melody, raising her hands for her friends to join in. Once again, one by one, her friends began to sing with her. Emily felt the familiar surge of power swirling through the three of them. Sparks flew off her rainbow jewel, and she saw the amber glow of Adriane's wolf stone. The music swirled and eddied around them, gathering energy as it grew. Huge snowflakes skipped in place, moving with the rhythm of the song, glowing with soft colors. Lorelei added layers of exquisitely sweet harmony in jewel-like chords.

The harpy kept the green horn raised, trying to draw in the magic. "Yes, send me your magic and I will use it!"

The song built, riding the crest of intense rhythmic waves. Energy thrummed all around them.

And Emily danced, twirling and spinning, feeling the music sweep her away. Her heart felt like it would break as she opened herself fully to the unicorn's feelings. She felt the pain and frustration, the sadness and shame, and the pure wonder and joy of their magical connection. The music skyrocketed into fireworks of power as she felt the strongest emotions ever from Lorelei. It wasn't a song of anger or hatred, it wasn't even a song of love that Lorelei sung. It was stronger, pushing the magic faster and farther than Emily could have believed possible. Emily spun faster, flashing on her own life—her father, sad and desperately searching for fulfillment; her mother, worried and afraid for her daughter—and suddenly she knew what she was feeling from the unicorn's music. It was a song of forgiveness.

Emily let the song ring out in a rush of feeling. The magic swirled, becoming a lightning bolt of power and slammed into the harpy, shattering the green horn into a thousand fragments.

The harpy screamed and collapsed amid the rain of glittering green shards.

Squinting against the blast, Emily saw Lorelei standing over the dark, prone form of the harpy. With a swirl of the unicorn's head, magic erupted from her crystal horn, spinning into the air. The sparkles formed a circle, and a portal opened before them.

The harpy scrambled to its feet, clutching its hand and cowering in fear.

"Destroy me, now," it hissed. "The Sorceress will, if you don't."

"Without the power of my horn, you are no threat."

"Why couldn't I harness it? Tell me!" the harpy begged.

"Some things cannot be taken."

"I don't understand."

"I know you don't. Be gone, harpy!"

"Allow me!" Ghyll hopped over and bounded into the harpy, knocking it into the portal with his big blue belly. With a nod of her head, Lorelei swirled the portal closed, leaving only slight wisps of blue smoke hanging in the air.

"Now, *that's* team work, frog boy!" Ozzie jumped up, slapping his paw against the flobbin's flipper.

Before she could catch her breath, Emily saw the unicorn walking toward her, white flakes drifting in her wake.

"Is this Avalon?" Emily asked, looking around at the wondrous landscape.

"This is a special place that I have found."

"I've seen it before, in my dreams."

"In friendship we are bound."

"I'll always be around," Emily finished, smiling.

"The dark creature will not hurt you anymore." The unicorn's musical voice was strong but anxious. *"But its evil work remains. I must repair what was destroyed."*

Suddenly Emily understood. *"You* didn't fail!" she told Lorelei. "The harpy destroyed the web, not you."

"You were right. Without my horn, I could not focus my magic."

"It's not your fault," Emily said. "The harpy used you. It tried to steal your magic." She knew that the harpy had used her, too. But Lorelei had forgiven her, even when the unicorn had almost given up on herself.

"So, the harpy tried to use your horn to force you to find Avalon," Adriane said.

"The Sorceress took my horn, but she could not harness its power. She gave it to the harpy, because like unicorns, harpies use musical magic."

"What would happen if the web wasn't repaired?" Kara asked.

"All worlds on the web would drift apart, no longer connected, and the magic would fade away, gone forever."

Emily bit her lip. Things sounded worse than she and her friends had imagined. They had all known that the Dark Sorceress was ruthless—that she would do anything to gain control of all the magic. She was so fixated on her goal that she didn't care who or what she destroyed along the way—even the web itself!

Lorelei gazed deeply into Emily's eyes. *"I must do what I was meant to—heal the damaged web."*

Emily nodded. "Tell us how we can help."

"You cannot stay on the web. It is not safe for you. Your place is at Ravenswood, Emily, with your friends."

"Can you get another unicorn to help you, to repair the damage before it's too late?" Emily asked.

Lorelei shook her head. *"Any of the others would need to leave their own areas unprotected."*

Lorelei's expression was anxious but determined. Magic danced from her horn, lighting up nearby snowflakes with bursts of color. With a wave of her head, she spun open another portal. Light from the swirling mist spilled over the pillowy bluish-white ground.

"Do you know where Avalon is?" Kara asked.

Everyone looked at her.

"What?" she said sheepishly. "Maybe she knows."

"Avalon has been lost to us."

"But you go there," Kara pressed. "I mean, the other unicorn I met took me there, to Avalon."

"A unicorn could surely take you somewhere to aid you on your quest, but no one has seen Avalon in centuries."

"So how come everyone thinks *we* can find it?" Kara wanted to know.

"You are mages." Lorelei's eyes sparkled. *"It is your destiny to find Avalon. Surely such wondrous magic can renew the web."*

"You could come back to Ravenswood," Emily suggested hopefully.

"I will return to my home, Dalriada. There are young

unicorns who must learn everything you have taught me."
Lorelei lowered her head and nuzzled Emily affection-
ately. *"About the power of healing—and friendship."*

"I will miss you." Emily hugged her friend.

"And I, you." Lorelei nodded to the portal. *"You must go
now, as well."*

"Um, I hate to intrude," Ozzie said. "But that thing
goes to Ravenswood, right?"

Lorelei shook her head. *"It leads to another nexus."*

"Then how are we gonna get home?" the ferret asked
anxiously.

Lorelei looked uncertain. *"Only a unicorn can navigate
the web . . . or . . ."* She trailed off, her song fading.

Emily leaned in closer. "Lorelei, what?"

The unicorn bowed her head. Her horn stretched
toward Emily. " *. . . or you must use the magic of a unicorn."*

For a second Emily wasn't sure what Lorelei meant.
"Your horn?" she cried.

*"The horn of a unicorn gives the one who possesses it magic
of any type she desires."*

"But it didn't work for the Dark Sorceress," Emily
said, confused.

"The sorceress took *the horn from me. It was never truly
hers. The magic of a unicorn can only be used when it is freely
given. That is our secret."*

Emily looked to her friends

"It's up to you, Emily," Kara said. "I couldn't keep my
unicorn jewel, because it was never given to me."

Still Emily hesitated, images flooding her mind. Lorelei broken and scared in the forest. The deadly, gleaming blade of the Dark Sorceress flashing ruthlessly down. The sickening, charred remains of the web where the harpy's evil music had destroyed its magic.

Then a different image flashed into her mind. Lorelei dancing across the web, repairing and strengthening it—doing what she was created to do, horn or no horn, filled with the magic that was inside of her. No one could take that away.

Taking a deep breath, Emily reached out and grasped the horn. A dizzying, jangling feeling overwhelmed her senses, and she felt like she was falling.

She opened her eyes and saw the horn sparkling in her hand.

"I am always here." Lorelei nudged Emily's chest with her nose, pressing against the beating of her heart.

She stepped back, reared, and raced away. With a mighty leap, she vanished.

"Good bye," Emily whispered, her heart twisting with loss.

"Come on," Adriane said. "Let's go."

She led the way toward the portal. Emily lifted Ozzie onto her shoulder and briefly patted Ghyll's warty neck. Making sure everyone was right beside her, she took a breath and stepped through—into darkness.

The blackness felt almost solid, as if it were pressing against Emily's skin. It was as if they had been transported to a place where light did not exist. Never had she experienced such total darkness. Her only solace was the horn she clutched tightly in her hand.

"I can't make my wolf stone glow," Adriane said, concerned.

"Me, either." Emily strained her eyes in the dark for even a glimpse of the rainbow jewel at her wrist.

It seemed the darkness had sucked the light even from their magic jewels.

"Stay close, everyone," she said into the void.

"That will be easy," Ozzie said, clutching her neck.

Emily thought about what Lorelei had told her. The magic of the horn had been given to her. It would bring what she desired most. "Keep us safe," she whispered, raising the horn high. "Lead us home."

The horn flashed in the darkness, and as her eyes adjusted, she saw that it was illuminating a path along a wide strand of the web. In the distance, pinpoints of light twinkled like diamonds strewn across velvet. She hurried forward, the others following behind, small specks on an infinite magical highway. Two pathways forked to the left and right. But which led back home?

Emily called to Lorelei for help. She felt a hint of the unicorn's presence and heard a brief echo of music. Light sparkled from the horn, pulling her, guiding her.

"This way," she whispered. She led them to the right, the horn casting long shadows behind them. Starlight sprinkled around them as more and more of the web beckoned in the distance.

"Ahh! Watch it, ferret! You tickled me!" Kara called out.

"That wasn't me!"

"Wasn't me," Ghyll said.

"Hey, that tickles!" Ozzie yelled.

"I felt something, too," Adriane said.

"Look, it's the horn," Emily said in wonder.

Long snaky strands flew off the horn. Emily tried to shake them loose. But as she waved the horn, more and more strands began to collect on it, like sparkling gold cotton candy.

The horn began to grow heavy under the weight.

"It's drawing strands of the web," Emily exclaimed.

"Well, hurry, it's falling all over us!" Kara cried, wiping wispy sparkling strands from her blond hair.

Emily picked up the pace, carefully following the ghostly path before her. "This way. Everyone stay together!"

Ahead, bright lights beckoned as dozens of pathways intersected—a nexus. At least a dozen portals floated silently around the platform.

"Which one?" Kara asked uncertainly.

Emily stood and stared, searching for the right answer. "I . . . don't know," she admitted.

"Well, if we end up in China, I'm going to be grounded for a year!" Kara said.

Emily closed her eyes and held the horn up high. She felt Lorelei's magic race through her. The newfound strength of her friend filled her with joy, love, and hope.

"This one." She pointed to a portal in the center.

Grasping hands, paws, and flippers, the friends stepped forward and leaped through the portal together.

16

"*O*oof!" Ozzie spluttered, landing on Emily's stomach with a thump. "Sorry about that."

"No problem." Emily set the ferret down on the grass. Glancing around, she saw that Kara, Adriane, and Ghyll had tumbled safely through the portal as well.

"*You're back!*" Stormbringer raced toward them, almost bowling Adriane over as she licked her face.

Adriane giggled and hugged the big wolf tightly.

Lyra ran to Kara and allowed herself to be caught in a big hug.

"Good thing I'm back," Kara said, inspecting the large cat. "You need a shampoo."

"*I let myself get extra dirty for you.*"

"Aww, how sweet!"

"Hey!" Ozzie called out. "It was no picnic for me either, you know."

Storm and Lyra walked to the ferret, each licking a side of Ozzie's face. Ozzie was lifted into the air by two giant tongues.

"*Akk!* Watch it, furballs!"

Loud cheers, squeaks, roars, and peeps rose over the field as the animals barreled in, crowding around the girls.

"They made it!" a brimbee yelled.

Emily, Adriane, and Kara took a bow.

"Your humble junior mages have returned," Kara announced. "And the harpy is gone!"

Louder cheers erupted from the group.

"Hey, what's that?" Ronif pointed to the portal.

The girls turned and gasped. Long, glowing strands spilled out of the swirling hole, piling up on the ground in a tremendous heap.

"It's strands of the web!" Adriane said.

"They must have come loose from the horn when we jumped through." Emily gazed down at the sparkling, clean horn in her hand. It was her last connection to Lorelei, and she felt a pang of deep sadness when she realized how much she would miss her new friend.

Pop! Pop! Pop! Pop! Pop!

The air exploded in colorful bubbles as five overexcited

dragonflies dove into the girls. They made a beeline line right for Kara's blond head.

"Oh, no!" Kara clamped her hands on her hair as the dragonflies zipped around her.

"Kaaraa!" Goldie ecstatically cried out, nuzzling into Kara's neck.

"Hi, Goldie." Kara gave the mini a scritch between her wings.

"OOoooOO!!!!"

Fred, Barney, Fiona, and Blaze swept past her and fell into the pile of glowing web strands. In a minute, strands went flying everywhere as the little dragons careened about, holding pieces in their tiny beaks.

Emily watched them with wonder. She looked at the horn. *Keep us safe.* She had wished for that with the magic of the horn. "That's it!" she cried out.

"What?" Adriane asked, ducking as Fred flew over, dangling a pile of strands.

"The strands! What better magic is there than the web itself to build a dreamcatcher?"

"You're right!" Adriane exclaimed. "Kara, do your thing!"

"You know," Kara retorted, "I'm perfectly capable of doing other *things* than playing with dragonflies."

"Right," Adriane agreed. "Just do us a favor."

"Yes?"

"Don't sing!"

Emily could not help giggling as she watched Kara stomp over to the pile of strands.

"Hey! D-flies! Front and center!" Kara called out.

"OOOooo, Kaaraa!" Fiona and Barney dove for her shoulder, fighting for position.

"Nuh uh! No cuddles! Get to work and start spinning!"

"Oookee dookee!" Goldie sprang into the air and started squeaking. The others buzzed with excitement, flocking over the pile of magic strands. Soon the dragonflies were busy weaving a new dreamcatcher.

"All righty then," Kara said, wiping her hands together. "Anything else?"

"Gee, let me think." Adriane scratched her chin thoughtfully.

"Um, guys."

The girls looked down at Ozzie. The ferret nodded over to the side of the field where Ghyll sat, hunched over and looking very sad.

Adriane and Emliy looked to Kara.

"What?" Kara stared back, then rolled her eyes. "Okay, let's get this over with."

Ozzie and the girls walked over to the depressed flobbin.

"Hey, big guy," Adriane said.

Ghyll looked up. "Oh, hi."

"Look," Kara began. "You helped us save Lorelei, and you did save me from falling into a bottomless void. So . . ." She puckered up. "I'll lay one on ya."

Ghyll looked down again.

"What's wrong, Ghyll?" Emily asked.

"I lied to you all, and I know it wasn't right."

"So why did you do it?" Emily asked.

"The Dark Sorceress turned me into a flobbin, and I thought she would turn me back if I helped her get the unicorn."

"What a chump!" Ozzie said.

"Ozzie!" Emily scolded.

"Sorry," the ferret mumbled.

"So I tried to get you to send it back. I know now that I was wrong. The Sorceress was using me just as she uses everyone and everything. When I saw *her*"—he gestured at Kara—"I figured with her magic, she might be able to change me back without having to get the unicorn involved."

"And cousin Brommy!" Ozzie said.

"I thought that if you liked me, you might help me and be my friend." The flobbin blinked his big eyes at Ozzie

"Ghyll, you made a mistake," Emily said. "We all do. But then you helped us. That's what counts. That's what makes friends." She smiled.

"I don't have any friends," the flobbin said sadly. "Who would like a flobbin?"

"Hey! I'm all puckered here!" Kara called out. "Last chance for a magic kiss!"

Ghyll turned sad eyes down to his big flippers. "I made

that up, too. There's no such thing as a magic kiss," he said dolefully.

"Oh, really?" Kara said, eyes narrowed. "You have no idea what you're dealing with, flubber. Girls? Shall we?"

Kara daintily held out her hands. Emily and Adriane stepped closer, allowing Kara to take their hands in hers. The wolf stone and the rainbow jewel flared to life, glowing with magical energy.

Bending over, Kara planted a kiss right on Ghyll's lumpy blue forehead. The flobbin's eyes went wide.

Sprlllloinnnnng!

A brilliant white burst of magic exploded into the air around them, hiding Ghyll from sight.

"Yaaak!" Ozzie cried. "What a kiss!"

Popping and sparking, the magic cloud swirled around Ghyll for a moment, then faded away . . .

. . . revealing a glowing purple figure the size of Ozzie. Dressed in a long, belted jacket and pointed shoes, the new Ghyll sported a humanlike face, shiny skin, and a long tail. He looked like a cross between an elf and a purple lizard.

Kara put her hands on her knees and bent down for a better look. "Little short for a prince."

"Well, I've been told I bear a striking resemblance to—woah!" Ghyll cried as he looked down at himself. "I'm back!"

"Hey!" Ozzie exclaimed. "How come you never told us you're really a spriggle?"

"I'm a spriggle!" Ghyll yelped. "You did it!"

Kara shrugged. "Okay, cool. You're not a flobbin anymore. Case closed." She wiped her hands and stepped away.

"You *are* a princess of magic!" Ghyll jumped up and down, stamping his small, pointed feet.

"And don't you forget it!" Kara said.

"How can I ever thank you?" Ghyll's purple ears quivered in joy.

"You can thank us just by doing the right thing," Emily told him.

"I will. I'll go back to Aldenmor and work with the mistwolves." He looked quickly up at Storm. "You don't eat spriggles, do you?"

"Not lately," the mistwolf replied.

The dragonflies were buzzing like busy bees, stretching the golden dreamcatcher tight over the opening of the portal.

"If you want to go, you'd better do it now," Emily told him. "Before it closes."

"With the web all messed up, how will I be sure I get to Aldenmor?" Ghyll asked.

Emily held up the unicorn horn. "Lorelei did say that I could have magic of any type I desire."

She pointed the horn at the portal and made a wish. "I wish for our friend to get to Aldenmor safely." The horn glowed, briefly followed by an answering flare from inside the portal.

Ghyll walked proudly to the portal.

"Hey, Ghyll!" Ozzie called out.

The spriggle turned to Ozzie. "Yes?"

"If you see Brommy . . ."

Ghyll looked at the ground, embarrassed.

"Give him my regards." Ozzie finished, and smiled.

Ghyll smiled back. "Will do." With that he jumped through the dreamcatcher and vanished into the mists.

"Well, this princess of magic is going home to take a six-hour bath," Kara announced.

"What are we going to do with the horn?" Adriane asked.

Kara eyed the glimmering jewel in Emily's hands.

"No, you can't wear it," Adriane said.

"I think it'd be best if we hide it in the library," Emily suggested. "Until we figure out what to do with it."

"Agreed," Adriane said. "That's the best solution."

Kara pouted. "Okay," she said at last. "But I still want a jewel!"

"Say, about this magic kiss business." Ozzie ran over to Kara. "You got another wet one in there?"

Kara swooped up the astonished ferret and spun around, planting kisses all over his furry head.

"*Gahh!* Watch the fur! Put me down!"

Adriane fell to the ground, laughing, her arms tight around Storm's neck.

Emily watched her friends and smiled. They had learned a lot about magic in such a short time, had seen its terrible potential for destruction and the wonder of healing and renewal. But most of all they had learned of its responsibility. The Fairimentals would be proud. In just a few months they had learned more about what it meant to be a mage than if they had apprenticed for years, not in the knowledge of spells and jewels, but something more essential, the truth in their hearts.

17

$\mathcal{E}$MILY OPENED THE door to the Pet Palace and slipped quietly inside. She hadn't seen Ozzie all day. Her mind flashed back to the disastrous scene with the dog food the other day, and she sighed, scurrying to track him down. If he made another mess, her mother would probably ship her off to boarding school and have the ferret stuffed. Besides, it was past time to do the afternoon feeding.

Emily heard humming. She hesitated, tempted to sneak back out.

But Carolyn looked up and saw her. "Em!" she exclaimed with a smile. "Come here, sweetie. Did you know your ferret could do tricks?"

"Huh?" Emily blinked, noticing for the first time that

Ozzie was standing on a wooden box, juggling liver snaps. He tossed them into the air, then one by one caught them in his open mouth.

She narrowed her eyes at him. He merely grinned in response, then did a backflip.

Carolyn laughed with delight. "You know, this is the smartest ferret I have ever seen. I just love him!" She grabbed Ozzie and gave him a hug. "You were lucky to rescue him, Emily."

"I know." Emily stared at the grinning ferret, thinking back to the day she and Adriane had discovered him caught in a trap in Ravenswood forest. That day had changed her life forever. And it never would have happened if her mother hadn't forced her to move to Stonehill. No matter how hard it had been to start a whole new life, she would never regret any of it. Ever.

She suddenly realized that Carolyn was watching her. With a flash of guilt, Emily remembered their argument again. How could she have said such terrible, hurtful things to her mother?

"Mom," she said softly, "I—I—"

"Yes?" Carolyn turned away from Ozzie, facing her daughter.

Emily took a deep breath. This was harder than she would have believed possible. Still, she knew she had to do it. She had to take responsibility for her own actions.

"I'm sorry," she said simply. "I acted like a total brat. I didn't mean to hurt you with those awful things I said."

Carolyn sighed and looked down at her hands. Then she took a step toward Emily. "I know," she said softly. "This move hasn't been easy for either of us. And I'm sorry, too—I had no idea how much you were hurting. You seemed so happy with your new friends."

"Oh, I am!" Emily put in quickly. "I really am. I guess I just wasn't as over it all as I thought, you know?"

Carolyn nodded. "You know you can always talk to me, no matter what's on your mind. And I'll do the same, okay?"

"Yes." Emily smiled and stepped forward into her mother's embrace. They hugged for a long, safe, comfortable moment.

"I love you, sweetie."

"I love you, too, Mom."

Rrrrrrrip!

"Ozzie!" Emily cried. Over Carolyn's shoulder, she spotted the ferret tearing open a fresh bag of liver snaps.

Carolyn turned and laughed. "Naughty, naughty!" she exclaimed, hurrying over to pull the bag out of Ozzie's grasp. "Come along, now. If you're a good boy, I'll let you taste my special vegetarian lasagna." She cradled Ozzie in her arms, then glanced at Emily. "School night. Don't stay out too late, okay, hon?"

"Uh, okay, Mom." Emily watched in surprise as her mother headed to the door with Ozzie. The ferret waved as he passed her.

Emily shook her head in confusion. Who ever would

have guessed that Carolyn would bond with Ozzie like that?

Oh, well, Emily thought. It's nice that Mom has a new friend, even if it is a wacky magical elf disguised as a ferret. Of course, that leaves me with nobody at all. She thought about Lorelei. They had become so important to each other in such a short time. They had healed each other, become friends. Why couldn't they stay together? After all, Adriane had Storm. Kara had Lyra. Who did Emily have?

Seeing that her mother had already filled the dogs' food dishes and taken care of the rest of her chores, Emily sighed and headed for the door. Outside, the reddish glare of the setting sun made her squint. As her vision adjusted, she saw two figures walking toward her across the lawn.

"Hey!" Kara called cheerily. "There you are. We were just thinking about walking into town for some ice cream. What do you say?"

"Yeah." Adriane added. "I need you to buffer-zone Miss Goddess of Magic. Her radiance is blinding me."

A feeling of warmth flooded through Emily. They understood. Her friends understood. They would be there for her, no matter what.

"Sure," she said.

They walked slowly back across the lawn. "So I'm totally psyched about the benefit concert," Kara said. "You'll never guess who's going to be the musical act."

Adriane shook her head. "No, but I'm sure you'll tell us."

"Well, what do you think about Be*Tween?"

"Yeah , sure," Adriane scoffed

"Huh? Huh? How cool is that?"

"I've heard them—they're really good," Emily said.

"They totally rock!" Kara exclaimed.

"And they're coming to Stonehill?" Adriane asked incredulously.

"Right into your backyard, baby."

"Wow, Kara. That's cool," Emily smiled.

"What are we going to do about Mrs. Windor?" Adriane asked.

"Oh, I'll take care of that. I'll send her free tickets."

"No way!"

As her friends continued to chat, Emily felt a flash of sadness mixed with pride. As much as she wished Lorelei could have stayed on Earth with her, she knew her friend had important work to do on the web. It was hard to accept that they couldn't be together—almost as hard as accepting her parents' divorce. It was going to hurt for a long time. Before encountering the unicorn, Emily herself hadn't even realized how deeply wounded she was. She had done such a good job of hiding her pain and sadness from everyone else that she'd hidden it from herself, too. She had been chasing an elusive ending to a song that needed to be sung. Now they both had to move forward, take what they had learned, and do their best to make things better.

Even though her father didn't live with her, it didn't mean he loved her any less. She would always carry the lessons he had taught her—and those still to teach—in her heart. Her mother's love would always be there, no matter how far from home Emily might journey. And her friends. Her wonderful friends who cared about her and supported her. That was stronger than any magic spell.

Emily took a deep breath of crisp autumn air, lagging a bit behind her friends. The sun had just dipped below the horizon, and the clear evening sky was growing darker with every passing moment. As Emily looked up, she saw that stars were starting to wink into sight here and there. Out of the corner of her eye, she spotted a flash of light diving toward the horizon—a shooting star.

Emily smiled up at it, still thinking about Lorelei. Their friendship was like that star—all too brief, but bright and unforgettable.

Thank you, she thought, hoping that somehow, some way, Lorelei would hear her and understand. *Thank you for everything.*

In return, she heard a faint, melodic whisper of a reply, like the distant echo of a shooting star's celestial song.

And it was perfect.

Bestiary &
Creature Guide

WOMMEL

AFFILIATION: GOOD

*W*ommels are red koala-sized creatures with thick fur and large eyes. They are native to the Moorgroves forests in Aldenmor. They appear cute and cuddly but Wommels are fiercely protective of their families. Working together, many wommels can provide relatively strong magic.

Pooxim

Affiliation: Good

*P*ooxim are sleek creatures that look like a cross between a songbird and a rabbit. They have a natural sing-song voice that conducts musical magic. The pooxim's thrilling songs of the wild can be heard echoing through the Moorgroves of Aldenmor, keeping the forests healthy and rich with magic.

FLOBBIN

AFFILIATION: NEUTRAL

*F*lobbins are large fairy creatures, rotund and frog-like. Fairy in nature, flobbins have a reputation for being schemers and tricksters. Flobbins are also natural magic trackers with a special knack for finding magic blobs, loose pockets of wild magic.

HARPY

AFFILIATION: EVIL

*H*arpies weave spells using musical enchantments. Not true shapeshifters, the harpy's music creates a beautiful vision, sort of a dream-time state— disguising it just long enough to get close so it can attack. Only those with powerful magic of their own can see the harpy's true form.

Rachel Roberts
on the Power of Healing

*E*MILY IS THE healer mage who learns healing isn't just about fixing broken wings. It's about being patient and listening. Supporting a friend who is sick can be very powerful medicine and you don't have to be a doctor or have a healing jewel to help. Being there with love and a fluffy pillow can make somebody smile. What really healed Lorelei was Emily's friendship. That's magic we can all practice.